FLEETING PASSION

Her scalp prickled as unseen eyes marked her passage, and Shadow became increasingly uneasy. She dodged into an alley—and collided with someone. Rough hands grasped her. She smelled leather and sweat, and sized up three large men surrounding her.

"Well, what's this?" the man holding her chuckled. "A ripe elvan piece, and so eager she ran right to us."

She glanced at the men, shrugging disappointedly. "Three, is that all?" she sighed. Shadow shook her head and started unlacing her tunic. "You three will just have to do."

She pulled open the tunic. The man holding Shadow had to release her as the garment was pulled over her head; then he stood gaping.

Shadow let the garment dangle teasingly from one hand. Abruptly, Shadow whipped the tunic into the face of the man who had grabbed her. She dived between his legs with a strong upward punch as she went and dash down the alley, ignoring the enraged shouts behind

S·H·A·D·O·W

Anne Logston

ACE BOOKS, NEW YORK

This book is an Ace original edition,
and has never been previously published.

SHADOW

An Ace Book / published by arrangement with
the author

PRINTING HISTORY
Ace edition / November 1991

ISBN: 0-441-75989-0

Ace Books are published by The Berkley Publishing Group,
200 Madison Avenue, New York, New York 10016.
The name "ACE" and the "A" logo
are trademarks belonging to Charter Communications, Inc.

PRINTED IN THE UNITED STATES OF AMERICA

10 9 8 7 6 5 4 3 2 1

To Mary,
who never stopped believing

ONE ═══════

It was midmorning when Shadow rode into Allanmere in grand style in a haycart, ragged, whistling and cheerfully broke. She jumped off at the Sun Gate and stood breathing the aroma of the city, a heady melange of baking bread, of tanning leather, of sweat and incense and dung.

A fruit vendor trudged past, pushing his heavily laden cart, and Shadow charitably lightened his load by two apples with the merchant none the wiser. Tossing one apple idly while munching on the other, Shadow gazed wistfully at a vintner's stall, then resolutely turned her eyes to the market ahead.

"Damn that Ragman and Filch," Shadow said mildly, feeding her apple core to the nearest horse. Bad enough that they had taken all her gold, leaving her bruised and unconscious by the roadside; bad enough that they had taken her expensive, hand-crafted tools and weapons; but did they have to take *all* of her wine?

Ah, but why waste her time on anger on this fine, sunny morning, when the great city of Allanmere lay before her as

1

fat and juicy as a pear ripe for the picking? Oh, life was grand!

Shadow dropped the second apple on the ground, rolling it underfoot until it was mushy, and scanned the market crowds at belt level—which, for her, was only a little below eye level.

"Hey, you." She snagged a filthy street urchin running by. "Do me a favor and I'll give you two coppers."

The boy eyed her skeptically.

"You got no money."

"I will if you do me the favor."

"Make it a Moon," the boy asserted.

"Half a Moon."

He considered.

"Done."

Shadow picked up the mushy apple.

"Go over there by that fruit stand and wait a few seconds. Then throw this at the man in the blue velvet tunic and make sure it hits him good. Then run."

The boy grinned and melted into the crowd. Shadow edged cautiously nearer, then loitered by a basket stand, waiting for the ruckus. No one would notice one more elf in this market.

SPLAT!

"What the—stop, you! Grab that boy!"

"Hey, off my foot, you oaf!"

CRASH!

"My pots! You broke my pots!"

"Watch out, you six-fathered idiot!"

"Watch yourself, you fumble-footed dolt!"

"My purse! Where's my purse?"

"Dung eater!"

"Hey, where's my—"

"Who's going to pay for my pots?"

"Son of a syphilitic cow!"

Shadow sidled back out of the crowd and walked non-chalantly into an alley, where she crouched behind a mound of refuse to inspect the contents of her now-heavy sleeves.

"Hey, how about my half Moon?" The boy was back, dirtier but grinning.

Shadow counted coppers, then shrugged and handed the boy a Moon.

"You need another favor, just ask for me," he announced importantly. "I'm Tig."

"Well, Tig, I'll add another copper if you can answer two questions," Shadow told him. "Who sells the best wine in the market?"

"That's easy." Tig grinned. "Master Walpert at the north end."

"And who sells the second-best?"

Tig thought for a moment.

"That'll be Master Ulm, over east by the slave stands."

Shadow surrendered the copper, waved at the boy's retreating back, and began searching for a fountain. She took a few minutes to scrub the worst of the grime from her hands and face, and pinned her thick black braids into a semi-orderly coil behind her delicately pointed ears before locating Master Walpert, who was busy stacking casks at his stall.

"Good day, master vintner," Shadow called.

Walpert turned, eyed Shadow's ragged clothing disdain-fully, and hefted another cask, his round face growing wine-colored with the effort.

"What do you want?" he grunted.

"Why, only a skin of your very finest wine, master." Shadow smiled, her large black eyes wide and innocent. "What will you take for it?"

Walpert paused briefly for a second look at Shadow's

clothing, sniffed disdainfully, and returned to his stacking.

"Five Suns—if you have it, which I doubt."

To Walpert's amazement, Shadow pulled a fat pouch from her sleeve and counted out five gold Suns, then shook her head and put them back.

"No, it's just not worth it." Shadow sighed. "It's a bit of a walk, but Master Ulm offered for three Suns."

Walpert's eyes hungrily followed the pouch back into Shadow's sleeve.

"That Ulm!" he growled. "He waters his wine daily to cheapen it!"

"That's as may be, friend," Shadow said regretfully, "but I'm not rich enough to spend five Suns when I can buy elsewhere for three. And after what he said about your wine being sold too young—"

"WHAT?" Walpert bellowed. "Young! I'll break his lying neck! Adar should wither his manhood, if it weren't too late!"

He fumbled for a skin and poured a mug full, thrusting it at Shadow.

"There, lady—taste that and learn the ripeness of Walpert's vintages!"

Shadow drained the mug in a remarkably short time, sighing in satisfaction.

"Ah, now there's a wine to warm the stomach," she said, nodding. "Ulm's wine did taste a little weak for all that, though he said you'd sell short because half your wine had soured—"

"*SOURED*!!" Walpert roared, his already-florid face darkening to an alarming hue. He grabbed a full skin and thrust it into Shadow's hands. "And him telling such lies in the very market! There, my lady—nay, I'll not have a copper of you! Drink it in good health, and tell your friends where the real wine is sold in Allanmere!"

"Oh, indeed I shall," Shadow agreed warmly. "Indeed I shall, Master Walpert, and Fortune favor you!"

Shadow looped the skin's strap over her belt and sauntered whistling back into the market, surreptitiously liberating a meat pie from its tray and munching contentedly. Oh, but the day was fine and life was grand! She swigged from the wineskin, paused a moment, then turned east.

"Ah, fair morning to you, Master Ulm!" she called.

TWO ═══════

It was late evening when Shadow walked into the Silver Dragon Inn, content and heavily laden, but so tired she could scarcely lift her feet. She gave the innkeeper three Moons for three days' board without even haggling, added another copper for a tub of hot water, and wearily climbed the stairs to her room.

Half an hour later, she relaxed luxuriously in her tub while a handsome bath boy scrubbed a week's accumulation of grime from her tanned skin. She eyed the boy appreciatively and he looked back as frankly, but she was so tired that even the prospect of a fine young man in her bed seemed more trouble than it was worth, and at last she sent him away with more than a little regret and a Moon in his pocket.

She toweled herself dry and attacked her wet hair with a comb, holding the ebony lengths up high so they did not trail on the floor, then braided and coiled it. The cool, wet hair felt good against the sore lump on the back of her head—souvenir of her farewell caress from former companions—and Shadow sighed happily, kicked her dirty

6

rags into a corner, and collapsed limply onto the bed. She pulled her pouch from under the pillow and tipped its contents out onto the blankets.

Despite the day's purchases, she still had fifty Suns, thirty-three Moons, and nearly fifty coppers. She poured them back into the pouch and picked up her last piece of booty to examine it.

It was a light, filigreed bracelet, silver by the look of it, and set with three deep blue-green skystones. The filigree was molded in delicately carved leaves, flowers and vines around its entire length, with supporting plate only at the clasp—which apparently was stuck, as it would not open. Perhaps the young man who'd been carrying it in his pouch had been taking it to a jewelsmith for repair.

Shadow chuckled again, sliding the too-large band on her own slim wrist. It would be worth a good many Suns on the market, or perhaps she would keep it against future poverty. She yawned broadly, tucked the pouch back under her pillow, and slid under the covers.

Time enough to worry later. For now, she felt as if she could sleep three days straight through, and she meant to try if she could do it.

She yawned once more, and the yawn ended in a snore.

When Shadow awakened, the sun was high and the clamor of the market came loud through her window. Shadow smiled and stretched comfortably, luxuriating in the sensation of cleanliness, and bounced out of bed to don the new tunic, trousers and boots she had purchased the day before.

As she bent to lace the boots, she realized that she was still wearing the silver bracelet. She frowned and pulled at it, then pulled harder, then, frightened, yanked at it hard. It remained closed around her wrist as firmly as if it had grown there.

Anxiously, Shadow peered closely at the bracelet. She could see no mechanism to release the catch. It wasn't all that tight. She could twist it around her wrist, and her wrist did not seem swollen; however, tug as she might, she could neither force the clasp open nor pull the band back over her hand.

A bespelled piece of jewelry intended to trap just such a thief as herself? Shadow thought a moment, then shook her head. No, not likely. No one could have meant an item of such obvious value to be stolen. And the man who had owned the pouch containing it—Shadow remembered him dimly—had been young and alert-looking, no easy mark; that was why she'd tried for the pouch in the first place. What challenge to steal from some numbwitted fool?

But it was she who'd been the fool, to vainly pop such a piece onto her wrist. Now she was at the mercy of whatever magic was in the bracelet, and she couldn't get it off.

Well, it didn't appear to be doing her any harm at the moment, and there were other concerns lined up for her attention this day—namely, the replacement of her wonderful tools, and the acquisition, by one means or another, of some weaponry. She could probably locate some metalsmith to cut the bracelet off, although it was a pity to ruin the beautiful filigree. She dismissed the bracelet from her mind, tucked her pouch of money into her sleeve, and marched downstairs for breakfast.

A copper bought bacon, ale and bread, and Shadow ate hurriedly before turning her steps to the market.

It was nearly midday before Shadow found what she wanted—an elvan metalsmith who dealt in finely crafted work. She inspected several different pieces while the proprietor, an unhappy-looking young elf, attended an irate human at the other end of the open-air booth. The elf was obviously distracted, and Shadow was sorely tempted to simply pocket her choices, but she restrained herself reluctantly; a metalsmith who made good thieves' tools was likely affiliated with the local Guild and under its protection. Finally the proprietor turned to her. His eyes brightened as he recognized a fellow elf, then widened as he noticed the large coil of Shadow's braids.

"Well! Fair morn, Matriarch," he said warmly. "How can I help you this fine, sunny day?"

"I'd like this set of tools," Shadow told him, "and these knives." She deposited the small leather packet and large stack of weapons into the surprised elf's hands. "How much for the lot?"

He quickly regained his composure and scribbled figures on a scrap of parchment.

"Twenty-two Suns, six Moons for all, Matriarch."

"Let me see that paper." Shadow quickly scanned the figures. "Come now, for such a large purchase, surely you can give me a better price than *this*. I'll give you fourteen Suns for the lot."

The elf grinned. "Ah, I'd sell them to my own mother for twenty Suns, Matriarch, but for you I'll beggar myself and give them away for nineteen."

"If you overcharged your mother that much she'd disown you, and I wouldn't blame her," Shadow told him. "Fifteen Suns."

The merchant opened his mouth to answer, but before he could speak, another voice interrupted.

"So this undersized elf fancies herself a fine warrior, eh?"

Shadow started at the voice, then turned to look at the newcomer. She found herself facing a tall, well-muscled human woman clad in leather warrior's garb, her eyes as black as Shadow's own, her dark brown hair confined in a single braid down her back.

"It's a sad day when humans dare to speak so insolently to their betters," Shadow returned tartly. "And sadder yet when they dare to interrupt an elf's bargain."

"Lady Donya—" the merchant began fearfully.

"Bargain, hah!" the woman interrupted again. "You couldn't bargain a sand flea into the desert. You want a bargain? Try this, then: match me in a game of dagger-toss. Win, and I'll buy your pretty toys for you; lose, and I'll stuff them down your throat. How's that for a bargain, eh?"

"Accepted," Shadow said loftily. "Finish fondling your money, human, for you'll soon be parted from it. Choose your target."

The woman picked a piece of blackened wood from a nearby fire and traced two targets on the wooden wall of a nearby building, then traced a line on the ground some distance away.

"There," she said. "Do try at least to hit the wall, if you can."

Shadow picked out three of the daggers she had selected for purchase and toed the mark. She flipped the daggers consideringly from hand to hand, trying to accustom herself to their balance, until an impatient sigh from the human woman returned her attention to the contest. Immediately she let fly, one after the other.

"Not bad," the warrior conceded, gazing at the three daggers grouped solidly in the center of the target. She drew three of her own daggers, toed the line, and threw. The daggers *thunked* solidly into the center of her target.

They both walked forward, eyeing the targets critically.

"The same," Shadow said at last. "Another round?"

"If you're determined to humiliate yourself." The woman shrugged. "On the same target this time?"

Shadow grinned.

"Let's make it interesting," she said. "Same target, same time, and offhand?"

The other scowled but nodded reluctantly. They lined up at the mark.

"Call it, my friend," Shadow said to the vendor.

"Now!" the elf called.

Six daggers flashed to the target, and after a brief pause, the competitors moved forward to judge their success.

There was a long moment of silence while the warrior frowned darkly at the target. Then she sighed and suddenly threw an arm around Shadow's shoulders.

"Ah, damn it," Donya complained. "I never *can* beat you."

"Bet on it." Shadow chuckled, giving her friend a hug. "By Macaran's withered pisswhistle, it's been almost two years. Where've you been keeping yourself?"

"Why, right here," Donya said surprisedly. "This is my hometown, didn't you know? I'm the High Lord's own daughter." She looked at Shadow suspiciously. "But what are *you* doing here?"

"Ah, that's a story demanding wine and a good meal to go with it." Shadow sighed.

"All at my expense, I'll wager." Donya laughed. "Well, I'll be taken in once more today, why not? Arick, wrap up Shady's goods and mind you've sold her your finest, understand?" She counted out Suns into the bewildered merchant's hand while Shadow picked up her package.

"Come on," Donya said. "I know a tavern where you can bite the ale right off at the neck of the bottle."

" . . . so when I left Overpass, I ended up stuck with Ragman, too." Shadow grimaced, tucking the last dagger into a boot sheath. "Those two—not a spark of artistry between them. Common highwaymen, that's what they were, and I got properly taken."

She emptied the last of the pitcher of ale into her mug, then drained the mug in one gulp.

"But you haven't told me—what about you?" she said. "And why didn't you ever tell me you're the daughter of the High Lord of Allanmere, eh?"

Donya shrugged, looking uncomfortable.

"I never thought it mattered much," she said. "I hadn't thought I'd be declared Heir, so I could pretty much do as I liked. I didn't really want people to know or they'd treat me differently—either hate me because I'm noble born, or fawn on me for the same reason. Anyway," she said quickly, changing the subject, "I can't believe you ended up taking two more losers under your wing. How many does that make it? Two dozen, three?"

"I'll know better next time, Fortune favor me." Shadow sighed.

"You," Donya said pointedly, "are entirely too kind a judge of character, and you *won't* know better next time, not as long as your soft heart keeps getting the better of your good sense. So, have you beggared every merchant in the marketplace, or did you spare a few for tomorrow?"

"Donya!" Shadow chided innocently. "How can you think such terrible things about me?"

"So there's still a few unsheared sheep?" Donya interpreted with a laugh. "Well, keep your sticky fingers out of my family's coffers, that's all I ask, and I'll keep my peace."

"Now, you know I'd never rob a friend," Shadow protested.

"Ha. I know if you got one look into the treasury, I'd be out in the market with rags and a bowl," Donya retorted. She glanced out the window. "It's getting late, and I've got to speak with my father. Why don't you walk me back? In fact, I could put you up at the castle, if you like."

Shadow shook her head regretfully.

"Better not put too much temptation in my path, Doe. Besides, I've paid ahead for my room. So tell me," she added, "what's the Guild like hereabouts?"

"Unpopular, in a word." Donya grimaced. "The Guildmaster, Ganrom, is a good enough thief by all accounts, but I wouldn't say much for his administrative sense. He's contracting openly with the Aconite Circle—the local brotherhood of assassins, which I'm not supposed to know about—and it's getting hard for the City Council to ignore him, tradition or not. Going to join up?"

"Maybe. I don't want some local pouch-cutter turning me in to the city guards."

"Then it might be a good idea, if you're planning on staying around for a while," Donya agreed. "Ever thought of settling down? You're good enough to make a try for a seat yourself, if you wanted."

Shadow choked on her ale, then laughed.

"Me? A Guildmistress?" she scoffed. "Fortune favor me, that's a good one, Doe. What kind of headaches are you trying to push me into?"

"Well, it was just an idea."

"Guildmistress," Shadow repeated, chuckling. "The Brightwater will flow backward first. But I may stay awhile. The pickings are good in the market. I think I can even survive without sizing up your family's purses."

Donya grinned back. "I'm sure my family will be vastly relieved," she said. "But listen, I really do have to go. Meet me here tomorrow for lunch? I'll pay."

"Bet on it." Shadow grinned. "How can I refuse a free meal?"

They walked north toward the castle, Shadow taking the

opportunity to ask Donya about how the city was arranged. She'd come in at the Sun Gate at the far east edge of the city, which passed through the city walls into the eastern part of the Mercantile District. The Mercantile District was split in the middle by the market. South of the Mercantile District, the city split into three parts—Middletown just south of the District on the west, Guild Row below that, and the slums of Southtown filling the southeast. North of the Mercantile District was the Noble District on the west side and the Temple District on the east, with the royal castle grounds sandwiched between and hugging the wall of Allanmere just beside the North Gate. The only other area of interest was the shipyard outside the city walls, commonly known as the Docks, where trade boats came to anchor.

They stopped at the castle's outer gates. After Donya had said her good-byes and gone in, Shadow hesitated outside for a moment, suppressing an urge to furtively check the place's defenses, but decided to visit the local chapter of the Guild instead. Whistling, she made her way back to the market—

—and found her arm seized in a grip of iron.

"You!" a voice snarled, and Shadow looked up into the angry brown eyes of yesterday's victim.

Shadow lashed out quickly with her feet, one smashing into the man's shin, the other to the groin. The young nobleman groaned and doubled over but retained his tight grip on her arm.

Shadow twisted quickly, ramming her elbow up into the man's face. He screamed and let go, his hand going to his spurting nose. Shadow darted quickly into the crowd, knocking over a fruit cart behind her, dove under a wagon, and emerged in an alley.

Shadow trotted down an increasingly complex maze of

alleyways until she was thoroughly lost, then grabbed a
passing urchin and waved a copper under his nose.

"Can you take me to Tig?" she asked him.

The boy grinned and the copper vanished into his rags.
He wordlessly grabbed Shadow's hand and scuttled down
the alley, ducking under laundry hung out to air, and
emerged in a small, filthy plaza inhabited mainly by
beggars. Tig was seated beside an incredibly ancient and
toothless human with a dirty rag tied across one eye and one
leg missing. Tig glanced over and grinned in recognition.

"'Lo, mistress," Tig shouted, nudging the old man.
"Uncle, here's that lady I said about."

The old man's single eye, a surprisingly bright blue,
twinkled delightedly.

"Ah, welcome, Matriarch. Come and sit with us, come
and sit."

Shadow squatted beside the two, patiently removing
Tig's hand from her belt pouch.

"Thanks for the welcome," she said, laughing, "but I'm
only 'Matriarch' when it lowers the prices. I'm Shadow to
the rest."

"Shadow, eh?" Uncle said thoughtfully. "Seems I've
heard that name about the market before, can't remember
where. What can we do for you, lady Shadow?"

"I need a name to go with a face," Shadow told him. "I
was going to ask Tig, but I imagine you see a good many
things, Uncle," she added slyly, dropping a Moon into his
bowl.

Uncle grinned toothlessly at the coin and made it disap-
pear into some recess of his rags.

"Now that's a fact, my elvan miss," he said. "The face?"

"This man's human, middling height," Shadow remembered. "Youngish, but I'm no good with human ages.
Brown eyes and hair, dark skin. He's a noble, dresses in

blue velvet. Arms are a sword and a wand crossed on a shield, scalloped edge."

"Oho!" Uncle cackled. "Those are the arms of the House of Batan. Tig, who's the young lord?"

"Derek, Uncle."

"Derek, that's the one," Uncle agreed. "A brash young bit, fancies himself a fine sword and always looking for excuse to use it. You'd do well not to run afoul of him, my lady Shadow."

"Too late," Shadow said ruefully. "But tell me, do you know a good, close-mouthed mage who doesn't mind dealing with the Guild?"

Uncle nodded. "You'll be wanting the lady Aliendra on Guild Row, she's close-mouthed enough and a fine mage. Works for the Guild now and again."

"Thank you, Uncle." Shadow dropped another Moon into the bowl. "Tig, here's a copper for you if you'll show me where the Guildhouse is, and this mage's shop."

Both were very prominently located in Guild Row. After paying Tig, Shadow hesitated, then decided on the Guild-house.

The building was old, dirty and shabby, filled with rough-looking characters—surprisingly few of whom were elvan—drinking at littered tables, gambling, or just sitting around. To Shadow's surprise, the clerk/barkeep led her to Guildmaster Ganrom himself, a smallish, sallow human with a long scar running across his chin. He was as dirty and shabby-looking as the building, and Shadow would have thought him some common highwayman but for the Guild-master's sigil hanging around his neck.

"So you're the new talent I've been hearing so much about," Ganrom said with a grin. "Supposed to register first thing, know that?"

"I didn't know where the Guild was," Shadow said

patiently. "I only got here yesterday. I can't very well march into every strange town asking, 'Excuse me, but where's the Guild of Thieves?' Anyway, I wasn't sure I'd be around long enough for it to matter. What's the fee?"

"Well, that depends, see?" Ganrom said. He fished three small bands from his pocket, one each of gold, silver and copper, and all engraved with the Guild symbol.

"Copper token, that's good for Southtown, Middletown, Docks and Market," he explained. "Silver token's good for the Mercantile and Noble Districts, and gold's good anywhere in Allanmere, see?"

Shadow raised an eyebrow and shrugged.

"Gold, then."

"Hmmp! Ambitious bit, ain't you, for being new to town?"

"Bet on it," Shadow said good-naturedly. "How much?"

"Twenty-five Suns. You got that?" Ganrom grinned skeptically. Then his eyes swept briefly over Shadow's trim form. "Or maybe you and I could work something out."

Shadow said nothing, but counted out the money and placed it in front of Ganrom.

"Hmmp!" Ganrom grunted again sourly. He gestured to the clerk.

"You! Get the elf a gold token and sign 'er up."

Shadow signed the register and accepted the inscribed band, slipping it over the tip of one black braid and pinning it back in place. Aware of Ganrom's annoyed frown, she hurried out of the Guildhouse and headed down the street, shaking her head in disgust.

That old fool! Not a question about her background or rank, and he was willing to turn her loose on the city. And three separate tokens! What idiocy! He'd spend thousands of Suns trying to enforce such limitations. Not to mention the bad policy of accepting fees "in trade," as he'd implied.

She at least hoped he was conscientious in fattening the proper purses among the local constabulary.

Aliendra's shop was full of the sweet, spicy, and pungent aromas of herbs and less pleasant tools of the mage's trade, all sold in neatly labelled flasks and bottles on numerous small shelves. Shadow gaped at Sunblossom oil, chuckled at powdered Passionweed root, wrinkled her nose at dried basilisk blood, and puzzled over several less recognizable components. Aliendra, a dark human woman dressed in gray, sipped tea behind the counter and watched Shadow impassively.

"How may I help you?" she asked at last, when Shadow had finished glancing over her wares.

Shadow made sure no one else appeared ready to enter the shop, approached the counter, and pushed her sleeve up to display the bracelet.

"Actually, this is rather embarrassing." She grinned. "I put this on yesterday and now I can't get it off. I have no idea what it is."

The faintest hint of amusement twinkled in the woman's eyes, although her expression betrayed only cool interest. She glanced briefly over the bracelet, not touching it.

"Is it yours?" she asked at last.

"It is now."

"Ah." This time Aliendra smiled slightly. "Come back to my workroom, and I'll see what's to be done."

A little hesitantly, Shadow followed the woman into a back room filled with books, weights, braziers, and other implements of less obvious function. Aliendra lifted down a huge, ancient volume and leafed through its pages, shaking her head thoughtfully. At last she closed the tome with a gentle sigh.

"Divining its nature is simple enough," she said, "but removing it intact may be less so if the enchantment is powerful enough. Are you willing that it be destroyed, if necessary, to remove it?"

"If you have to." Shadow shrugged. "It looks valuable, but I'm rather more fond of the hand."

"A pity. Its workmanship is wondrous." Aliendra clasped her hands around the bracelet, closed her eyes, and whispered a short incantation of which Shadow understood not a word. For a moment Aliendra's hands glowed golden; then the glow died.

Aliendra sighed again and released the bracelet. Then she looked at Shadow strangely.

"Do you trifle with me, elvan lady?" she asked slowly. "Why did you bring this here? Do you threaten or challenge me?"

"I don't understand."

Aliendra opened her mouth, then paused and shook her head.

"No, I will not become embroiled in this matter. Please leave my shop, and do not return. There is no fee."

"Wait, now," Shadow protested. "You said you'd—"

"Go!" Aliendra frowned threateningly, but Shadow was amazed to see more than a little fear in her eyes. Shadow bit back an angry retort and stalked out of the shop, blinking in the sudden sunlight.

Shadow ducked into an alley to study the bracelet again. It appeared innocuous enough, surely nothing to frighten a mage of Aliendra's repute. It turned easily around her wrist and felt comfortable there. The leafy design was reminiscent of elvan work, now that she looked at it, as was the delicacy of the silver filigree. Likely it *was* elvan work, and perhaps Aliendra had a grudge against elves. And that raised another question—what was this Derek fellow doing carrying a piece of elvan magic? And he had valued it highly enough to pursue her for it, which meant he had at least an inkling of its nature . . .

Hmmm. That carried interesting possibilities, but it was late and she was tired. Shadow rolled her sleeve down over the bracelet and headed back to the Silver Dragon, where this time she was not too tired to let the bath boy earn his Moon.

Shadow slept late enough that there was barely time to trifle with the market before noon. Donya was waiting at the tavern, but Shadow pulled her friend back toward the stalls.

"I smell roasting dragon," she said, licking her lips.

Donya sniffed the air and grimaced.

"Your nose is keener than mine," she said. "All I can smell is dung and whores' perfume."

"There!" Shadow said triumphantly. Not far ahead, a large firepit had been dug, and a huge haunch was roasting on a gigantic spit turned by six mules. Three slaves, overseen by a fair, well-muscled warrior, brushed sauce over the cooking meat.

"Good day, Dalin!" Donya called to the warrior. "I see your hunt met with success."

The warrior smiled broadly and nodded at the meat.

"Only a small one," he replied. "But the battle was fine, my lady. You should've been there."

"I wish I had," Donya agreed. "But at least I can enjoy the fruits of your battle. What'll you take for two rare slabs?"

"Ah, for you and your friend, I'll take not so much as a copper," Dalin said firmly. He deftly sliced off two thick chunks of meat, skewered them on sticks, and dunked them into the sauce, handing the sticks to Donya and Shadow.

"I don't believe I've had the pleasure," he said, glancing at Shadow.

"I'm Shadow and the pleasure's all mine." Shadow grinned, appraising the man's fine physique. She bit into the chunk of meat, sighing contentedly as the delicacy burnt its way down to her stomach.

"What luxury," she said. "If your fighting skills are as great as your culinary art, friend Dalin, I hope the dragons don't get word of it; else every dragon in the lands will flee to the hills."

Donya nudged Shadow sharply and prodded her away from the warrior, who was beaming at the praise.

"You might as well save your flattery." Donya chuckled. "He's sworn to celibacy."

Shadow glanced back in amazement at the handsome warrior.

"What a tragedy!" she sighed. She bit again into her chunk of dragon.

"At least he can cook," she amended.

"So how are you enjoying Allanmere?"

"Mmmmp. Do you know a fellow named Derek, House of Batan?"

"Dimly." Donya shrugged. "He's come to a few functions at the castle. Thinks a lot of himself, as I recall. Why?"

"Does he have any special involvements with the elves hereabouts?"

Donya snorted.

"Not likely. A bunch of elf-haters, that's what the Batans are. Derek himself had a run-in with the Guild back when Evanor held the seat, challenged one of the elvan apprentices to a duel, but Evanor spirited the fellow out of town."

"Now, that's interesting," Shadow mused. "Tell me, do you know any really good mages hereabouts? Besides Aliendra on Guild Row, I mean."

"A few." Donya gave Shadow a curious look. "My mother's quite good herself. What's this about, Shady?"

Shadow glanced around, then showed Donya the bracelet.

"I stole it from this Derek fellow yesterday," she said, "and it won't come off my arm. I took it to Aliendra—"

"She's good, really good."

"Maybe," Shadow said disgustedly. "But all she did was tell me to get out of her shop. Wouldn't tell me a Fortune-be-damned thing. It looks like elvan work to me."

"It certainly does." Donya shrugged. "I can't imagine why Aliendra wouldn't tell you what it is, seeing that you're stuck with it anyway. Why don't you dine at the castle this evening and ask Celene about it? Maybe she can tell you more."

"That's what I was hoping. But why would one of these elf-hating Batans have it?" Shadow pressed.

"I can't imagine an elf selling Derek dung off his bootsoles, let alone a valuable piece of elvan magic," Donya said dubiously. "Likely he killed an elf in a duel and claimed it as challenge-spoil. I'll see if I can learn anything, if you like."

"If you can." Shadow shrugged. "But enough about that. Where's the best brothel in town? I'll treat."

Donya burst out laughing at the change in subject.

"Well, *you* haven't changed, Shady. But here in town, I'm the High Lord's daughter, my friend, not just any warrior. I can't go about having tumbles in a brothel."

"So we take them to an inn?" Shadow asked innocently.

"That's not the point. I just can't do that kind of thing around here. It'd make problems for my father."

"I don't know what your father has to do with it," Shadow grumbled. "Unless you're saving yourself for *him*."

"Shady, don't you ever worry about anything besides filling your purse, your belly, and your loins?" Donya demanded with an exasperated sigh.

Shadow grinned placatingly at her friend.

"What else is there?" she teased. "Have you discovered some interesting new vice? Tell me!"

Donya had to laugh.

"Come back to the castle with me," she said. "Let your loins wait a few more hours, and I'll introduce you to the best dreamweed merchants in Allanmere."

"Now, *that's* a bargain," Shadow said, pleased.

"The best dreamweed merchants in Allanmere" were a stunningly handsome, tall, silver-haired elvan man and an elvan woman whose coil of dark hair was as tall as Shadow's own. They ran an herbal shop in the eastern Mercantile District, far from the general clamor of the market. The shop was quiet, exquisitely decorated, and filled with every plant or fungus-derived substance Shadow had ever heard of.

"Good afternoon, my lady Donya, and to you, kinswoman," the man said. "How may my sister and I serve you this afternoon? We've some fine new teas from the south, just in on the last caravan."

"I'm not buying today." Donya smiled. "But I wanted to steer my friend's business your way. Shadow, this is Argent and his sister Elaria, two of the smoothest tricksters in the city."

"Tricksters?" Elaria smiled gently. "Why, my lady, when have we ever bested you in a bargain?"

"Every time I've been in here, as well you know, my friend." Donya laughed back. "But you'll find Shady here a harder mark."

Shadow tore her eyes away from Argent and examined the jars of dreamweed in all its various forms. Glancing at

Elaria for permission, she picked a disk of dreamweed resin from one jar to sniff it.

"Oh, come now," she chided. "You can do better than *this*."

Argent's brown eyes twinkled back at her.

"Indeed we can. Sister, we have a discriminating customer today."

He reached under the counter and withdrew another jar.

"We prepare this ourselves," he said, "and don't sell it openly, as many humans find it too potent."

Shadow sniffed the disk offered her, then smiled approvingly.

"Fortune favor me, *this* is the good stuff," she said. "I'll take an ounce, plus a pouch of your finest leaf."

Donya leaned against a wall and watched in amusement while the elves bargained for the better part of half an hour. Finally she interrupted.

"Oh, please," she begged. "The three of you would squeeze a copper till it bled. Argent, settle for twenty Suns and I'll throw in dinner at the castle tonight, if you'll escort Shady and keep her out of trouble."

"Go on." Elaria smiled to her brother. "I'll mind the shop."

"Why do I feel I've been taken to the very limits of my purse?" Argent laughed. "Very well, then, kinswoman Shadow. I am escort and guardian, and pauper as well."

His gaze on Shadow, despite his words, was entirely approving.

Shadow had been as far as the castle gates the day before, but not inside; this time, however, she could not help but be impressed. The castle sat against the north wall of the city, overlooking the northeast loop of the Brightwater River, and was surrounded on the other three sides by sweeping lawns and gardens. Donya, Shadow and Argent were met at the outer gates by six stony-faced guards, who followed them to the castle doors before surrendering them to the house guard. From there they were escorted to the dining hall where, according to Donya's page, Lord Sharl and Lady Celene would join them shortly. Two guards remained in the room, flanking the door.

Shadow sat down gingerly at the long wooden table, drawing a dagger and tossing it nervously from hand to hand as she gazed in wonder around the room. Thick tapestries, embroidered in silver and gold, softened the severity of the stone walls, and soft lanterns in crystal sconces cast a gentle light over the room. At the foot of the table, a huge fireplace drove out any evening chill. Other than that, the only feature of note in the room was the huge inlaid table itself, surrounded by twenty chairs. The furniture was sized for humans, and although most elves would have been comfortable enough, Shadow's shoulders barely rose above the tabletop. Shadow stared at the silver tableware and tossed the dagger a little faster.

"Now, now," Donya whispered. "You promised."

"I know," Shadow said irritably. "I was a fool."

"And put that dagger up. You're making the guard nervous."

"Have some wine," Argent said diplomatically, filling Shadow's goblet from a nearby decanter.

Shadow drained the goblet at a gulp and went back to tossing the dagger.

"Lord Sharl and Lady Celene," one of the guards announced from the doorway.

Shadow turned hurriedly for her first glimpse of real royalty, then stifled a chuckle. Donya's parents were, after all, only Donya's parents, and resembled not a bit what Shadow would have pictured as a High Lord and Lady of a huge city.

Celene was young for an elf married to a human—judging by the length of her dark brown hair, she was perhaps a decade or two younger than Shadow, though, like most elves, she was much taller—and had the same deep brown eyes and firmness of expression as her daughter. Sharl was middle-aged by human standards, his own dark hair beginning to gray at the temples. Looking at him, Shadow could see the source of Donya's striking, strong features and muscular height. Both he and his lady were simply dressed in tunic and trousers which, but for their fine material and the House insignia at the shoulder, could have clothed anyone in the market.

Donya gave her mother a warm hug, bending down a little to do so, and then beckoned Shadow and Argent over.

"Mother, Father, this is Shadow, an old friend," she said. "And you already know Argent."

"Welcome, Argent, and to you, Shadow." Sharl smiled. "It's rare that we meet any of Donya's associates from her travels. Sometimes we think she's ashamed of her parents."

"More likely she's ashamed of her associates," Shadow corrected with a chuckle.

"Donya has spoken of her friend Shady many times," Celene said, her warm brown eyes twinkling merrily. "I feel that we know you already."

Shadow raised an eyebrow.

"What did she say?"

"Let it suffice," Celene said, chuckling gently, "that I wonder if I shouldn't count the silver before you leave."

Shadow laughed and followed them to the table where, to her surprise, Sharl and Celene sat by Donya, Argent, and Shadow rather than in the traditional seats at the head of the table. Shadow knelt rather than sat on her chair so she could reach her plate, then grimaced with some embarrassment as an over-efficient servant quietly brought a cushion.

"Oh, we observe the formalities when we entertain the nobility." Sharl shrugged at Shadow's curious glance at the seating arrangement. "But tonight, at least, we can sit where we can hear you without having to ask you to shout. At most dinners of state, the screaming matches are bad enough that we occasionally resort to messengers. And my lady—"

"I was thoroughly sick of it all." Celene chuckled. "And so at one dinner with the heads of several Houses and influential members of the City Council—it was quite formal and stuffy, you know—I loosed a cage of pigeons in the room, and told everyone to tie messages to their legs! My, but you should have seen the faces of some of those lords and ladies."

Shadow burst out laughing at the image of the pigeons— and the probable consequences thereof.

"Oh, my," she gasped. "I'd have given my last copper to have seen it."

"Well, it wasn't so bad as Father's idea." Donya grinned. "He threatened to make them tie messages to rocks and toss them across the table."

Servants unobtrusively passed platters and bowls on the table and refilled goblets. Shadow sternly suppressed an urge to pinch the over-dignified serving lad nearest her.

"Ah, you can just leave that here," she told the wine steward, relieving him of the bottle from which he'd refilled her goblet.

Donya helped herself to roast fowl.

"Mother, do you have to sit in audience this evening?" she asked.

"I don't remember." Celene frowned, glancing at her husband. "Whose turn is it tonight, dear?"

"Sorry, I've lost track." Sharl sighed.

Celene shrugged, drawing a small but sharp dagger from a sheath at her waist.

"Your call, then, dear," she said, then flipped the dagger adroitly into the air.

"Ummm—hilt!" Sharl said, eyes riveted on the dagger.

The dagger spun brightly end over end and dropped to embed its tip firmly, point first, into the tabletop.

Celene smiled brightly at Donya.

"Sharl's in audience tonight," she said.

"Next time *I'll* flip the damned dagger," Sharl grumbled.

"Fine, dear," Celene said serenely. "Then I'll *know* to call 'hilt.' Which reminds me, the Council of Churches has got up another petition to expand the Temple District."

"Well, there's nowhere to *put* any more temples, expansion or not," Sharl said explosively. "Where does *he* suggest another be squeezed in?"

"I believe he mentioned the northeast end of the Mercantile District, dear."

"There isn't room there for so much as a pushcart, and they know it," Sharl growled. "Damned if I'll listen to another lecture from that robed swindler Vikram. We can't expand the Temple District short of renegotiating the Compact and moving the wall, and damned if I'll do that just for them. I can't keep the bloody elvan delegates awake and sober long enough to get the renegotiations I *need*—no offense meant to anyone present," he added quickly, glancing at Shadow and Argent.

"And none taken." Shadow chuckled. "Fortune favor me, how did you ever find elves to sit on the City Council?"

"He told the elvan leaders that if they didn't send someone to represent their interests he'd pass every anti-elvan bill brought before the Council." Argent smiled. "Now every Matriarch or Elder has to serve a one-month rotating term on the City Council, or find someone else to do it for them. They pay the most exorbitant sums for fellow elves to sit in for their turns."

"What about you?" Shadow asked. "Have you ever done it?"

Argent shook his head quickly.

"I'm not qualified," he said with a tone that sounded suspiciously like relief. "Since I own a business in Allanmere, I'm taxed as a citizen and would have a biased interest."

"It all sounds like a lot of bother to me." Shadow shrugged.

"Oh, it is," Celene agreed with a sigh. "And the saddest of it is that most citizens think Sharl and I less harassed than they, while in fact we were lucky to make time to conceive Donya when I became fertile."

"But I thought—" Shadow began, then paused. Elf-human marriages generally produced twins, and then only if the human partner was fortunate enough to be alive during the elf's rare times of ripeness. Donya had never mentioned any siblings— She shook her head. It was certainly none of her business.

"You thought?" Celene prompted, but there was a hint of pain in her expression. Sharl was studying his plate, and even Donya did not meet her friend's eyes.

"I thought it was impossible to get an elf *that* interested in politics," Shadow finished smoothly. "How ever did Lord Sharl manage?"

"He never has, actually." Celene chuckled, her frown fading. "I'm a pathetic High Lady, positively pathetic. However, it's in the city's Compact that one ruler be human and the other elf, and I'm afraid Sharl bears the brunt of the politics."

Shadow's eyebrows raised as she looked consideringly at Donya.

"Somehow I can't picture you in the job." She grinned.

"The thought doesn't quite thrill me," Donya said wryly. "Neither does trying to find an elvan husband and settling down now, after all those joyful years of wandering about and trying to get myself killed."

"There are other ways," Sharl said kindly. "If Donya doesn't wish to rule, Celene can remarry when I die."

Celene made a rude sound, startling Argent.

"Or Sharl could father an heir elsewhere and have the child legitimated," she said flippantly.

"Celene, as I've told you before—" Sharl began, his lips set.

"And as *I've* told *you*—" Celene retorted with equal stubbornness.

"Mother, could you stop arguing long enough to consult for a little while with Shadow?" Donya said gently. "She's got—"

Donya paused and glanced at Shadow.

"Would you rather I kept it private?"

"From your father and Argent?" Shadow shrugged. "They'd find out anyway. No, it shouldn't matter."

With a few promptings from Shadow, Donya told Celene the story of the bracelet and Aliendra's odd behavior.

"But you've got to *promise* to tell me what it is," Shadow said. "The curiosity is killing me."

"You put me in a difficult position, kinswoman." Celene frowned. "As a mage and a fellow elf, I want to help you. But as Lady of Allanmere, I worry that Aliendra, a reasonable mage, would refuse to tell you what the bracelet is. I worry what I might loose upon my city."

Shadow shrugged. "Eventually I'll find a mage who'll take my coin and help me," she said indifferently. "If it'll weigh on you, never mind."

"How about this?" Donya suggested. "Shady, would you

promise that if the bracelet would actually pose a *danger* to the city, that you'll either give it up or take it elsewhere?"

"All right, I can promise that," Shadow said after a moment's thought. "If it's actually dangerous, that is. Anyway, I can't see a piece of elvan magic being that dangerous."

Then it was Celene's turn to consider.

"Very well," she said at last. "On that basis, I see no difficulty. Shall we move to my workroom?"

Argent laughed.

"The reputation of your laboratory considered," he said, "I believe I'll watch Lord Sharl take complaints from the people."

"What did he mean about the reputation of her laboratory?" Shadow asked Donya furtively as they followed Celene out of the dining hall and down some stairs. "I don't want to lose my arm, you know, or find myself turned into a swamp-croaker."

"Oh, no, Mother isn't some mad alchemist." Donya chuckled. "It's just that she's been doing some experimenting with plant magic over the years, and occasionally it gets out of hand. Last month she tried an antiquated spell and all the wooden bedsteads on the upper floors sprouted. I'm afraid the story got all over town."

Celene's workroom was as neatly stocked as Aliendra's shop, if smaller and not as well supplied. Shadow glanced quickly around and was relieved to see no evidence of past mishap—sprouted table legs, perhaps, or ominous charred circles on the ceiling.

With some difficulty, Celene lifted a small silver anvil out of a box and placed it on the table beside a silver hammer.

"There we are," she said, wiping sweat from her forehead. "Put the bracelet on the anvil and we'll see if we can't get it off your wrist, at least."

"Wait, now," Shadow said warily. "I don't want anything smashed. My hands are my livelihood, you know, and I've grown rather fond of them over the centuries."

Celene grinned mischievously.

"Don't worry," she assured Shadow. "I do know what I'm doing. I haven't lost a hand yet."

"Neither have I," Shadow grumbled, "and I'd just as soon keep it that way." Reluctantly, she laid her braceleted wrist on the anvil. "What now?"

"Presently I'll tap the bracelet with this hammer," Celene explained. "When I do, simply lift your hand up and away from the anvil. You may feel a slight tingling, but that's all."

Celene closed her eyes, holding the silver hammer loosely in both hands, and began chanting steadily. Shadow realized that both her sweaty hands were clenched tight; she relaxed them with effort.

At last, with infinite gentleness, Celene lowered the hammer until it touched the bracelet. A delicate chiming note reverberated through the room, growing in volume until Shadow's sensitive ears ached. Quickly, she lifted her hand up; to her amazement, the bracelet passed *through* her wrist, or her wrist through the bracelet, with nothing but a warm tingling sensation, so that the bracelet remained on the anvil.

Celene laid down the hammer, made one final gesture, then sighed contentedly.

"It worked!"

"I'll say it did," Shadow muttered, rubbing her newly liberated wrist. "How did you manage that?"

"It's a question of affinities," Celene said absently, inspecting the bracelet. "I merely persuaded the bracelet that your hand was no longer there. Hmmm, this is interesting."

Shadow and Donya leaned to look over Celene's shoulder—Donya bending, Shadow on her tiptoes.

"What is it?" Donya asked.

"There's some script on the inside of the clasp," Celene murmured, squinting. "It's terribly faint and worn. Definitely elvan, though—Old Olvenic, I believe—ah! 'Aufrhyr.' That's 'open'."

"Fortune bless the maker," Shadow said sarcastically. "He tells us what it *won't* do. But what *will* it do?"

"You're right, that is ridiculous," Celene admitted. "And altogether too obvious. But perhaps—put it back on, Shadow."

"I just got rid of the Fortune-be-damned thing," Shadow protested, but she slid the bracelet once more over her wrist.

"Now touch the clasp and say 'aufrhyr,'" Celene instructed.

Shadow shrugged and obeyed. To her surprise, the clasp clicked open, releasing the bracelet.

"Well, that's useful," Shadow said grudgingly. "A magic lock. At least I can take the thing off now."

"You don't understand," Celene exclaimed delightedly. "I can see why Aliendra—oh, my, this *is* a devious bit of work."

She glanced rapidly around the room, then picked up a small locked box.

"Now, touch the lock—no, with the hand with the bracelet—and say it again."

Sudden understanding brought a grin to Shadow's face, and she reached out to touch the lock.

"Aufrhyr," she said, and an audible *click* sounded from within the lock.

Shadow opened the lid, then shut it, grinning even wider.

There was a long moment of silence.

"Well," Donya said at last, weakly, "you *did* promise to stay out of the family treasury."

Shadow laughed, polishing the bracelet against her tunic.

"You don't have anything to fear from me, Doe." She chuckled. "This is a pretty trinket—and useful, too, no doubt—but where's the challenge? Start to lean on this and before long I'm overconfident and careless. No, thank you. My wits and skill and Fortune's favor have served me well enough so far, and I won't trade them for a magical crutch."

"Then what will you do with it?" Celene asked slowly. "I admit I'm relieved to hear you speak as you do, but will you sell it to another, or destroy it?"

"Oh, no, lady," Shadow said, shaking her head wonderingly. "I'm not parting with this pretty. I've got my professional pride, but you never know—no, indeed."

"Well, I'm satisfied," Donya declared. "Don't worry, Mother. Shadow's honest in her own way." She grinned. "Once I knew what it was, I knew she wouldn't use it, anyway."

Shadow raised one eyebrow.

"Is that a challenge?"

"No." Donya laughed. "Just faith in the ego of a master artist, that's all."

"Now, you both keep quiet about this," Shadow warned. "I don't want every copper-token cutpurse in the town sharpening his knife for my throat. And they would be, too."

Celene nodded slowly.

"Yes . . . at least now we know who has it," she said. "Very well, I'll say nothing even to Sharl, for unless it is badly misused it is none of our concern."

"There's one thing that worries me, though," Donya said more seriously. "What was Derek Batan doing with it? How did he get the bracelet, and did he know what it was?"

"I'm interested in that myself," Shadow agreed. "Hmmm. Might be worth a little checking around." She shrugged. "In the meantime, though, I could use some more of that excellent wine."

"Yes, and Sharl will be wondering if I've blown us all to the northern wastes." Celene smiled. "Best we reassure him."

Argent was found in the main receiving hall of the castle, where Sharl, now dressed uncomfortably in full regalia, was arguing heatedly with two gray-robed priests. The foremost of the two, a tall, elderly man whose craggy face was for the most part concealed behind a crinkly white beard, wore the sigil of the head of the Council of Churches. His associate, a shorter, rotund, middle-aged fellow, stood slightly back and nodded sagely all the while, occasionally leaning to murmur something quietly in the bearded priest's ear.

"Ah, Celene, there you are," Sharl called before they could sneak back out. "Come here for a moment, will you?"

"Yes, dear." Celene sighed resignedly.

"Tell me, my lady," Sharl said with exaggerated patience. "In your opinion, do you think the elves are likely to grant us an additional fifty acres on which to build an external temple enclave?"

Celene's eyes twinkled, although her face remained solemn.

"That would be outside the Compact, dear," she said. "However, if the enclave would be willing to pay a separate tithe to the elvan tribes—I imagine it would be in the area of sixty percent of gross income—perhaps the chieftains would consider granting the land rights on a private basis."

"There you are." Sharl beamed. "Shall I arrange a meeting with the elves, my lord Vikram? Bobrick?"

Vikram, the elder priest, took a mere two or three hundred words to back down, and Celene retreated hastily during his soliloquy.

"Poor Father," Donya said sympathetically as soon as they were out of earshot. "The Council of Churches will hound him to his funeral pyre. Not a day's peace he's had in a month."

"I think he enjoys it." Argent chuckled.

"Of course he does," Celene said warmly. "He's never happier than when he can be angry at them, and they always oblige. Do you know, one of those new sects actually denounced him publicly for having a 'heathen' wife?"

"Father's too tolerant." Donya frowned. "I'd have banned that sect from town."

"And you'd have made a serious mistake," Celene chided. "Freedom of worship is guaranteed, so long as the temples obey the Compact and the city's laws. If your father began banning sects out of personal dislike, the others would chew him up and spit him out. Let a sect squawk as it will; it gains only enemies by maligning a ruler otherwise popular with the people. And speaking of the people—" She glanced at Donya.

"Oh, nothing serious." Donya shrugged. "Some grumbling about the new hunting ordinances, but I think everyone knows the elves were getting tired of chasing poachers out of the Middle Zone. Somebody broke into the Temple of Charbad and stole a golden ewer; a clumsy amateur job, but the temples are upset about it. Probably some two-copper thief trying to impress someone."

"Oh, so you're the royal ear-to-the-ground?" Shadow teased. "I'll be more careful what I say."

"Someone must keep Sharl and me advised of the public opinion," Celene said. "Citizens don't always feel free to voice their complaints in royal audience, and we can't afford to wait until a problem becomes a crisis. Argent has been helpful on occasion, also. Many people who won't speak to the daughter of the ruling house will talk freely to a shopkeeper."

Shadow shrugged, grinned, and resolved that *she* wouldn't talk too freely!

"Now, a thief, with connections to all sorts of people—" Celene began.

"Oh, no," Shadow said firmly. "Wait just a minute. If you're looking for payment for your spell work, I'll pay in straight gold. But I'm trusting my life to a blunt dagger if the Guild thinks I'm chattering to the law."

"I wasn't speaking of spying against the Guild," Celene said persuasively, "only of listening for rumors of trouble. We would, of course, be willing to pay you for your assistance."

"Yes, and the Guild would pay me, too," Shadow said ruefully, "with a knife in the back."

"She's right," Donya said. "Shady's new in town, and the Guild always suspects a talented newcomer. She may be in danger just for coming here tonight."

Shadow shrugged.

"Let them wonder what I'm up to," she said. "I don't mind. But—your pardon, Lady—I'm a Guild member, and I like to keep my priorities straight. Doe's saved my life more than once, and I wouldn't refuse her or her family much, but my loyalty doesn't sell for coin."

"I'm afraid Shadow's right, Mother," Donya agreed. "But as far as owing me, Shady, I'd question your accounting. If anything, I owe *you*. Mother, remind me to tell you sometime about the time Shady and I were waylaid by a pack of bandits down south in Everfar and she—"

"Oh, Fortune favor me," Shadow mumbled, blushing. "Not *that* one, will you?"

"Why, Donya." Celene smiled. "I do believe you've succeeded in embarrassing your friend."

"Now I'm curious," Argent said. "What *did* Shadow do?"

Donya laughed.

"I guess I'd better keep my mouth shut," she said. "Get her drunk enough and she'll tell you herself."

"From what I've seen of her drinking, that might be an heroic task." Argent smiled. "Well, kinswoman? May I ply you with wine and dreamweed?"

"As long as *you* don't get too drunk," Shadow said mischievously. "I want you able to take full advantage of my helpless condition."

"What a subtle invitation!" Argent laughed. "Very well, kinswoman, may I offer you some very traditional hospitality?"

"If Donya and her family don't mind our rudely abrupt departure." Shadow grinned.

"Not a bit," Celene said laughing. "Go ahead and make off with Argent while the evening's still fresh. All I ask is this: I want to hear that story someday, too!"

Argent's house, a stately building in the western Noble District, seemed to Shadow hardly less luxurious than the castle itself. Having asked where she could freshen up, she was escorted to an in-ground bathing pool, from which bubbling water sent up a gentle cloud of steam. Shadow timidly dipped a finger into the water, which, to her amazement, was only pleasantly warm.

"How does this work?" she asked. "Is it magic?"

"Not now," Argent told her. "The town is built over several mineral springs deep in the earth, similar to those that empty into the swamps to the north. When the town was built, conduits to the springs were magically bored, and now many buildings have access to those conduits. You should have seen the bathing pools at the castle if this one impresses you."

Shadow pulled off one boot and stuck her slender foot into the frothing water.

"Whoosh!" She giggled. "That tickles." She pulled off the other boot, then attacked the lacing on her tunic.

"Shall I meet you in the parlor?" Argent asked politely.

Shadow pulled off the tunic and flung it into the corner.

"Whatever for?" she asked innocently. "Why don't we just have our wine in here?"

"In the pool?" Argent asked, raising his silver eyebrows.

"Why not?" Shadow laughed. "Maybe we'll find an interesting new way to drown."

THREE ≡≡≡

Shadow awakened by slow, luxurious degrees: first came awareness of the softness of the sheets against her skin, then the enticing aromas of sex and wine and hot food, then the gentle touch of sunlight on her closed eyelids.

She opened her eyes, stretched slowly, and grinned. Argent was still asleep beside her in a bed which could have accommodated twelve people on intimate terms. Otherwise, they were alone in the huge stone room, but some servant had quietly placed a tray of breakfast on the table not long ago.

Shadow slid out of bed, gently pulling some of her hair out from under Argent, and tiptoed over to the table. After a peek under the dish covers, she trotted back to the bed and shook Argent.

"Wake up," she said, tickling his ribs. "Breakfast is here." Her tickling fingers moved lower. "Or would you rather skip breakfast and go directly to dinner?"

Argent's eyes flew open and he grabbed Shadow's hand, rolling swiftly over to pin her beneath him.

"You," he said firmly, "are a merciless vixen. Can't you even give someone time to wake up properly?"

"Well, I was working on waking you up properly," Shadow teased. "But I thought you might like some breakfast first."

Argent sighed.

"Shadow, some of us have shops to run and can't spend the whole day in bed, much as we might like to."

"Argent, Argent," Shadow scolded, "you've become too citified. Elves shouldn't run businesses. They start getting their priorities mixed up."

Argent laughed and rose, releasing Shadow.

"I think Allanmere is going to be an interesting place to live while you're here," he said. "Will you be staying in town long? I'd like to see more of you."

"I think you saw about all there is to see last night," Shadow said, grinning. Then she shrugged. "As to how long I'll be here—who knows? The market's as good as any I've seen. After the ridiculous sum I paid for a Guild token, I might as well get some use of it."

"It's a pity," Argent mused. "The Guild certainly isn't what it once was. It used to be more reputable—more profitable, too—when Evanor held the seat."

"How did an oaf like Ganrom ever gain the seat anyway?" Shadow asked. "He didn't seem very smart, and he can't have all that much support in the Guild, from the talk I've heard."

"The usual way," Argent said. "Killed Evanor. Or had him killed, more likely. Ganrom's done a lot of business with the Aconite Circle—the local assassins. Every thief who seemed likely to challenge him since then has turned up dead. It's been rumored that Ganrom has some powerful backer."

"Well, it's no concern of mine." Shadow shrugged. "I

certainly won't spend much time around that pesthole of a Guildhouse." She smiled sweetly. "Maybe I'll spend more of my time in the Mercantile District, instead."

"Shadow—" Argent began warningly.

"I know, I know." Shadow sighed plaintively. "I've got to quit making so many friends, or before long there won't be a pocket in Allanmere that's fair game. Anyway, with a couple of possible exceptions, I don't burgle fellow thieves."

"I'm not a thief."

"Ha!" Shadow found her tunic neatly folded at the foot of the bed and slid it over her head. "After what I paid for that dreamweed, you are. But I'll admit it's the good stuff."

"And I've got to go sell some more of that good stuff," Argent said firmly. "Eat some breakfast, and I'll walk you as far as the market."

"No, I'll walk you to your shop." Shadow grinned. "I think I'll have a look at the Temple District today."

Argent raised an eyebrow.

"Aiming high, aren't you?" he said. "I'd take care if I were you. The Temple District's had a rash of robberies lately, and a known thief isn't safe in the area."

Argent might have been right; however, in her new tunic and freshly scrubbed skin, her braid coiled elaborately and pinned with gold, Shadow looked like any moderately wealthy elf of station and not at all like a thief, and she was new enough in town that word of her should not yet have spread outside the Guild. No one took notice of her as she strolled through the district, feigning disinterest at what was going on around her.

The Temple District was every bit as busy and interesting as the market, if not more so. The priests were fat and wealthy, their costumes elaborate and often ludicrous, and arguments between priests of different sects were loud and often quite amusing.

Many ceremonies were performed publicly in the front plaza of each temple, and these ceremonies ranged from revolting to entertaining. At the Temple of P'andar, a prophet was reading the entrails of a sheep; Shadow wrinkled her nose and hurried on before he could complete the ceremony, at which time the entrails would be scattered over the worshippers.

At the Temple of Grurg, two acolytes caught fighting had been set the penance of publicly battling out their differences, their weapons being two large and smelly fish. Shadow and several others watched the amusing spectacle for some time, until the smell became too much.

At the Temple of Bodri, five temple handmaidens, clothed only in bejeweled ornaments, were doing a ritual dance of some complexity, the object of which seemed to be to make the most possible noise with the jangling jewelry. A large group of men, including priests from other temples, were gathered there to discuss the respective attributes of the five women, who seemed not the least disturbed by the various comments, suggestions and propositions shouted in their direction.

Shadow paused in front of the Temple of Ebraris. Its sigil, executed in exquisitely realistic marble statuary, depicted two men and a woman engaged in a marvelously complex sexual maneuver. Shadow grinned. The ceremonial activities of the very popular Temple of Ebraris were entirely to her taste, and she was momentarily tempted to visit the temple where, for a small donation, she would be made very welcome indeed; but if she was observed, it would endanger her neutral status. Shadow sighed, giving the temple one last, longing look, and walked on.

The Temple of Urex, as was its custom, was carting away the roasted carcass of its sacrificial bull, which would be cut up and distributed to beggars in the market. The passing cart reminded Shadow that it was lunchtime, and two coppers bought her half a roast fowl from a passing vendor. Then she noticed a crowd gathering by a platform at the very center of the Temple District, and wandered over to investigate.

A very dirty, ragged male human was being dragged onto the platform by four robed men. A fifth was heating up a brazier, and three more were following in procession.

Shadow picked out a human standing nearby and nudged him.

"What's going on?"

The man awarded her a brief glance.

"Temple of Urex found this fellow pilfering out of the offering box." He shrugged. "When they searched him, they found a Guild token on him."

"Aren't thieves supposed to be turned over to the city guard?" Shadow asked.

The man gave her another glance.

"New in town, are you?"

"Mm-hmm."

"Criminals caught inside a temple are turned over to that temple," the man told her. "Long as it ain't murder, that is. The temple can inflict about anything short of death."

"Why didn't the Guild ransom him?" Shadow frowned.

The man chuckled wryly.

"From the Council of Churches? That's a good one, little sister."

Shadow scowled, but said only, "What'll they do with him?"

"Cut off his hands, I reckon." The man shrugged again.

Shadow shook her head ruefully, then frowned as two of the robed figures stepped forward. She recognized the two priests who had been arguing with Lord Sharl the night before.

"Let this worm's punishment serve as a warning to that festering sore in Allanmere known as the Guild of Thieves!" Vikram shouted, waving his arms at the crowd. His face purpled with the passion of his speech. "May our example show all the people of this fair city what should be done with such scum who live as parasites, stealing the sustenance of others!"

Suddenly there was a loud scream, drawing Shadow's attention back to the unfortunate thief. His captors had forced his face into the brazier, and his screams continued for a few more moments before he slumped, unconscious.

"Nope, I guessed wrong," the man beside Shadow said.

Shadow caught a glimpse of the burned face as the thief was helped, staggering, off the platform. She grimaced, looked distastefully at her roast fowl, and tossed it aside as she walked away, leaving High Priest Vikram to continue his impassioned speech.

As the smell of burned flesh faded behind her, Shadow mentally shrugged the incident off. Hard luck for the thief, of course, but a burned face could be healed cheaper than severed hands, and he still had his livelihood. And any idiot worth his token knew you didn't burgle offering boxes; picking the priests' pockets was much more profitable, and easier, too. The thief had been a fool, plain and simple, and deserved what he got. Still, there was something about the incident nagging at the back of Shadow's mind . . . oh, well. She'd worry about it later. Meanwhile, she was beginning to regret throwing away her lunch. It was after midday, and she was getting hungrier all the time.

Shadow located a vendor hawking cheese-and-meat pies and unobtrusively relieved him of three, smiling contentedly to herself. Her first theft in the Temple District!

She was a good deal less content after a few more hours' walk. Since she was wearing no temple's emblem, she was fair prey for every initiate. She was threatened, coaxed, bribed, challenged, lectured, and once physically dragged toward a temple. The priest, however, finally accepted a refusal in the form of two fingers asserted painfully into his eyes.

Disgusted, Shadow retraced her steps with the aim of leaving the rather disagreeable district. Leaving was more difficult than entering the Temple District, since evening was coming on and worshipers were flocking in for sunset rituals. Shadow paused outside the Temple of Urex, watching as High Priest Vikram and his assistant—Bobrick, that was it—ushered in the citizenry to worship.

Shadow frowned. Bobrick had glanced her way, then taken a second look—and now was staring directly at her, hatred unmistakable in his expression. Shadow gave him a sweet smile and walked on, troubled.

What grievance could Bobrick, an officiant of the Temple of Urex, have against her? He couldn't know she was a thief.

Then Shadow smiled. Of course, he'd seen her when he and Vikram had been harassing High Lord Sharl at the palace. Likely he thought her affiliated with the High Lord in some way, perhaps an informant, maybe even one set to watch him. No wonder! Shadow put the man out of her mind and hurried on, eager to return to the more entertaining bustle of the evening marketplace.

She paused briefly at the Temple of Fortune, occasioning more than a few startled glances from the acolytes. Elves worshipping the Goddess were rare indeed; the local elves, for the most part, worshipped the Mother Forest or not at all. Today there were more offerings in the bowl at the Goddess' left hand, offered by the unfortunate to propitiate the Goddess' dark side. Shadow herself felt that her luck had been pretty good so far; she tossed a Sun into the bowl at the Goddess' right hand in thanks, nodded casually at the statue, and hurried out of the temple.

She had hardly set foot in the Mercantile District before the prickling at the back of her neck told her that she was being followed, and very skillfully at that. She idled at this shop and that, hoping to catch a glimpse of her follower, but whoever it was stayed nicely hidden. Only her keen senses, aided by years of finely honed thieving instincts, assured her that she was, indeed, under surveillance.

Scowling, Shadow walked into Argent's shop, making sure that there were no other customers present. Argent himself was not in sight, but Elaria was restocking a few jars.

"Good evening, kinswoman." Elaria smiled. "Surely you aren't back for more dreamweed yet? Or are you looking for my brother? Go on back if you like; he's in the office."

Too annoyed for polite conversation, Shadow gave Elaria a nod of thanks and ducked through the door behind the counter.

"Good evening, Shadow," Argent said absently, squinting over a sheet of figures.

"What's that?" Shadow asked as she peered over his shoulder.

"Shop accounting." Argent frowned. "I think one of our suppliers is cheating us dreadfully, but I can't quite catch it."

"Look under 'Miscellaneous Freight'," Shadow told him. "Listen, is there a back door?"

"Miscellaneous . . . by leaf and vine, I think you're right!" Argent exclaimed. "How did you know that?"

"One thief knows another," Shadow said mysteriously. "Actually, to be honest, that's where *I'd* put it. The back door?"

"Right there, through the storeroom," Argent said, pointing. "Why?"

"There's someone following me," Shadow told him. "I want a good look at whoever it is. Listen, do me a favor, will you? See who comes in the shop after me and try to get a good look. And if anybody asks about me, I'd like to know about it."

"Why would anyone follow you?" Argent asked curiously.

"That's what I'd like to know." Shadow scowled. "Listen, I've got to go before they get suspicious. Just keep a lookout."

"Certainly."

Shadow ducked out the back door, glanced to the right and left to see if she was observed, then darted into the maze of alleyways at the south fringe of the market. The failing light and piles of refuse slowed her progress more than she liked, but she hoped she had lost her follower; she was nearly lost herself in the twisting ways. She emerged at a point not too far west of the herbal store and glanced down the street, but there were too many people and it was too dim to see much. She shrugged and gave up, and headed back into the alleys to take a roundabout way back to the inn. At least she was reasonably sure there was no one behind her now.

The feeling of being followed did not return, but Shadow grew increasingly uneasy in the maze of alleys. As the sun set, disreputable-looking types were emerging from buildings into the dim passages, and she was aware that eyes watched her from behind shutters and through cracked doors. Here, her "wealthy elf" image was no good at all; rather, she had changed from an anonymous passerby into an appreciable target.

Shadow hastened her steps, then stumbled and nearly fell

as her foot connected solidly with something soft. Her feet skidded on the suddenly slippery bricks and she flailed wildly for balance. At last she recovered and glanced down to see what had nearly tripped her. She looked again, then swallowed hard.

Even in the dim light she recognized the burned face of the thief she'd seen in the Temple District, but he hadn't died of his burns. His throat had been slit so deeply that his head was nearly severed, and blood had pooled across the alley.

Shadow grimaced, but squatted to look. Other than the burned face, the slit throat—done by a very sharp knife, by the look—and a few older bruises, he hadn't been injured; no time to fight, then. She rifled his pockets and pouch, finding nothing but his gold Guild token. Something about that bothered her vaguely, but she was too worried to ponder on it; she pocketed the token and trotted on, grimacing at the soggy slapping sound of her wet boots against the bricks. New boots tomorrow, bet on it!

Her scalp prickled as unseen eyes marked her passage, and Shadow became increasingly uneasy. This was territory she knew nothing about, and she was going to get lost if she wasn't careful. She paused to estimate which way led back to the market, dodged into a west-facing alley—

—and collided with somebody; or rather, three somebodies.

Rough hands immediately grasped her and lifted her right off her feet. She smelled leather and sweat, and her keen vision sized up three large human men surrounding her.

"Well, what's this, what's this?" The man holding her chuckled. "A ripe elvan piece, and so eager she ran right to us!"

"Them elvan sluts just can't get enough, I've heard." Another laughed. "Reckon we'll have to oblige her."

"Well, oblige me on the ground, will you?" Shadow snapped, not struggling against the crushing hold on her arms. "I'm no good to you two feet in the air, and squeezing my arms half off's no way to put me in the mood!"

The man holding her laughed and set her down, maintaining a firm grip on one shoulder.

"There you are," he said. "That's better, eh?"

"Much." Shadow rubbed her sore arms. "Gods, fellows, all you had to do was ask."

She glanced at the men, shrugging disappointedly.

"Three, is that all?" She sighed. "Fortune favor me, hardly worth the trouble. Couldn't you come up with one or two more?"

"Huh?"

Shadow shook her head and started unlacing her tunic.

"Well, you ought to know it takes at least five or six humans to satisfy an elf, let alone a regular at the Temple of Ebraris," she said exasperatedly. "If you had any idea how long I've been looking—well, never mind. You three will just have to do. Come on! Who's first, or shall I take you all on at once? What're you all waiting for?"

She pulled open the tunic.

The man holding Shadow had to release her shoulder momentarily as the garment was pulled over her head; then he stood gaping incredulously before turning to attack his own clothes. The other two were already working on their pants.

Shadow carefully worked her arms out of the tunic sleeves, then let the garment dangle teasingly from one hand. The men stared raptly for a moment, then redoubled their efforts on buttons and lacing. Abruptly, Shadow whipped the tunic into the face of the man who had grabbed her. She dived between his legs with a strong upward punch as she went—answered by a howl of pain—and dashed headlong down the alley, ignoring the enraged shouts behind her.

Her eyes were adapting to the darkness, and she let intuition tell her which turns to take. The men had the advantage of longer legs, however, and they knew the area, which Shadow did not; and while her pursuers were not gaining ground quickly, they were gradually closing on her. Time to take a different road.

Rounding a corner, Shadow quickly scanned the alley and picked a wall, jumping for a high windowsill. Toes and fingers scrabbled for purchase, and she scrambled onto the roof and flattened herself against the slate tiles, quieting her breath with difficulty. Tiles slid under her feet to shatter on the bricks below.

A moment later the men rounded the same corner and paused. Shadow held her breath and froze, afraid she might knock loose more slate. To her relief, the men continued on, and Shadow slumped back against the cold slate to catch her breath. Well, she was lost in a strange and unsavory neighborhood without a tunic, but the situation could be worse. She could have lost her pants as well. All in all, she was mightily pleased with herself as she crawled up the steep slope of the roof.

From the rooftop she had a much better vantage point, and she could see the lights of the market not far to the west. On the way, she snatched a scarf from a clothesline and tied it around her small breasts, and stepped back out onto the road with a sigh of relief.

She was tired from her busy day, but it was far too early to think of retiring. She wandered through the market after buying a new tunic, not bothering much, and in an hour was richer by a few Suns. She was contemplating, from a distance, a fat merchant's equally obese belt pouch when her reveries were broken by a tap on her shoulder. At the same time, she became aware of a truly horrendous stench.

"Not him," a male voice said quietly from the direction of the awful smell.

Shadow looked over her shoulder to see a male elf only a few inches taller than herself, merry green eyes twinkling from behind an unruly mop of pale brown hair. A pipe in his mouth appeared to be the source of stench. Behind him was a second, fairer elf of unusually tall and stocky build—at first glance he could be a short human—otherwise bearing a striking resemblance to his companion.

"What do you mean?" she asked unconcernedly.

"Got a trap-spell on his belt." The elf with the pipe grinned. "I've seen it happen before. Stick your hand fast, it will."

He glanced about, then flashed a silver Guild token which vanished just as quickly into his pocket. "I'm Aubry, and this is my cousin, Cris."

"Shadow." She nodded. "And thanks."

She glanced at Cris, who was staring rather dumbly at her.

"Doesn't he talk?"

Aubry elbowed his cousin.

"Say something."

"Oh." Cris blinked. "Hello, Matriarch."

Shadow estimated the portion of her anatomy currently in Cris' field of vision and sighed.

Aubry pointedly ignored his cousin.

"Word's gone out to keep an eye on you," he told Shadow. "I think you must have made Ganrom nervous."

"Can't imagine why." Shadow shrugged innocently. "Listen, I'm in the mood for an ale or five, and I'm flush at the moment. Interested?"

"Why not?" Aubry grinned.

Shadow learned from Aubry that Guild members frequented a tavern called the Three-Spangled Horn at the edge of the market nearest Guild Row. The Horn was as nearly neutral territory as anyplace in Allanmere, the city guard well-paid to ignore it, and there was an unspoken law that no thieving could take place within its walls. The prices themselves were theft, but the ale was excellent.

Cris merely sat listening and toying with their lamp while Shadow and Aubry talked, feeding splinters into the flames, but a few pitchers of ale soon loosened Aubry's tongue.

"The Guild's fallen out of favor since Evanor—uh—retired," Aubry explained in answer to Shadow's question. "Used to be the Guild ransomed, but that's mostly stopped since Ganrom took the seat. Not that the Council of Churches would charge anything reasonable anyway," Aubry added quickly, "but Ganrom just gave up on it altogether."

"Well, then, by Fortune's muddy feet, what am I paying my Guild dues *for*?" Shadow said exasperatedly. "Certainly not the upkeep of that slimebox of a Guildhouse, bet on it."

"Shhh," Aubry said, glancing around nervously. "Keep your voice down. Ganrom doesn't like folk criticizing his policies. Especially very competent folk, you see? And *very* especially competent elvan folk. Cris, will you leave that lamp alone before you set the damned place on fire?"

Shadow raised an eyebrow.

"Ganrom's got a problem with elves? I wouldn't have thought so; he made a rather plain comment when I registered."

Aubry shook his head.

"Not that," he said. "It's that since Evanor—well, died, most of the elvan support has been withdrawn from the Guild. Used to be, two of three ranking thieves were elvan; now it's maybe one in five. There was a lot of uproar from the city elves when Ganrom took over, and now every time he sees an elf working towards high rank he thinks it's the start of an elvan push for the seat. Most of the high-ranking elves turn up dead or missing, sooner or later." He puffed thoughtfully on his pipe.

Shadow coughed and fanned the air, then reached for her mug.

"What's your angle?" she said at last.

"Hmmm?"

"Well, you're telling me all this," she said patiently. "Do you have a reason, or are you just trying to poison me with that cloud to make life easier for Ganrom?"

Aubry grinned amiably and shrugged.

"Let's say I've got an eye to my future prospects," he said. "Ganrom's bound to lose the seat sooner or later."

Shadow sighed and shook her head.

"Fortune favor me, you, and Donya," she said wryly. "Look, Aubry—I'm just passing through, filling my pockets. I'm not interested in making any trouble, and certainly not in getting into any. A few days or weeks, and I'm gone."

She was silent for a moment, lost in thought.

"Listen, how good are those musicians?" she asked suddenly.

"Pretty good," Aubry shrugged. "Why? Do you want something special played? I'll ask."

"No, I think I'll do it myself." Shadow sniffed. "At least it'll get me out of this reeking cloud of yours."

Shadow walked over to the lead player, an aged elf with a dulcimer, and waved a Sun under his nose.

"Know anything traditional?" she asked.

" 'Wind and Water'?" the elf asked after a moment's thought.

"Fine."

Shadow closed her eyes and composed herself as the

long-familiar rhythm began. Her feet had half-forgotten the patterns, her hands the motions, but slowly she remembered, letting the music carry her.

She was not aware when the conversation in the room slowed and died; her mind filled with smoky memories, the old aching joy that became a knot in her throat and threatened to spill from her eyes. How long it had been since she'd heard familiar music, danced the steps she'd learned so long ago!

Awareness of the tavern faded, and it was as though she danced in the forest again, her feet treading on hardened earth rather than stone, the leaves rustling overhead, moonlight rather than firelight illuminating her body as the songteller sketched the rhythm for the drums, and other dancers rose to join the pattern—

There was a metallic clinking sound, then another, then more. Shadow sighed, let the illusion slip away, and opened her eyes. The musicians had stopped, as had her feet, and the clinking sounds she had heard were coins being thrown on the floor at her feet. Most of the customers in the tavern had gathered in a semicircle around Shadow and the musicians, applauding, cheering, and throwing coins.

Shadow grinned without embarrassment and swept up the coins from the floor with an exaggerated bow. She handed a Sun to each of the musicians, bowed again to her audience, and hurried back to her table, waving for another pitcher of ale. This time Aubry's blank stare nearly mirrored Cris'.

"I thought you were supposed to be new in town," Aubry said at last, filling Shadow's mug from the fresh pitcher. He relit his pipe, to Shadow's disgust, and two nearby patrons hastily retreated to another table.

"I am." Shadow shrugged, accepting the mug. Nearly

half the ale disappeared in one gulp, leaving Shadow's mouth mustached with foam. "Ah, that douses the fire."

"Come on, now," Aubry coaxed. "I know better than that. That dance you just did is native to the forest tribes in the Heartwood, and what's more, hardly any of *them* dance the traditional stuff anymore. If you didn't learn that dance here, where did you—"

Shadow held up a silencing hand.

"Keep your voice down, will you?" she said mildly. "I said I was new in *town*. When I left the Heartwood, Allanmere wasn't much more than a few farms and a grazing common."

"The city walls were built over three hundred years ago," Aubry said thoughtfully. "But still, there are elves older than that. Surely someone would've recognized you by now."

"I doubt it," Shadow said, shaking her head regretfully. "My folk lived near the Western Heart—hmmm, they're calling it Songwater now. I left just after my first century and a half, and most of my clan were killed during the Black Wars fifty years later."

"But that would make you over fifty decades old," Aubry protested.

"Five hundred forty-two, if you're counting," Shadow corrected. "I know, I know—don't look a year over five hundred, right? Thank you, thank you."

She placed the last coin in her pouch.

"Not bad," she said. "Sixteen Suns, twenty-five Moons, and a dozen-odd coppers over what I gave the musicians. My dancing must've improved with age."

"I wish your singing would," a familiar voice stated as Donya joined them at the table. "Have either of you fellows heard her sing? Well, then, Fortune's favored you so far."

"I," Shadow said with dignity, "have the voice of a lark."

"A tone-deaf lark."

"You should talk!"

"And I do," Donya agreed. "But I *don't* try to sing. And I see your judgment hasn't improved with age, either, Shady. After that performance, there isn't a thief in the Guild who won't know your face."

She grimaced.

"Phew, what's that stench? Smells like a three-day-old battlefield on a hot day."

Shadow shrugged. "Ganrom has everyone watching me anyway. Ten eyes or fifty, what of it? At least this time they saw what I wanted them to see. Aubry, put out the pipe, will you, before the barkeep throws us out?"

"Sorry," Aubry said sheepishly, extinguishing his pipe.

"You," Donya told Shadow sternly, "are looking for a slit throat."

Shadow swallowed the rest of her ale and waved for more.

"I don't have to look," she said cheerfully. "I already found one tonight without trying."

"What!" Donya blinked, and even Cris abandoned the lamp momentarily to glance at her.

Shadow shrugged.

"I saw a thief who'd been caught burgling the Temple of Urex," she said. "They burned his face and let him go, but I stumbled over him in the alley not much later. He was wearing a new ear-to-ear smile."

"I heard Pim was caught in the temple," Cris said unexpectedly. "I didn't hear what had happened to him. He wasn't a very good thief." He turned back to the lamp, staring into the flame.

"Pim was a two-copper thug and nothing else," Aubry

declared. "But I can't imagine anybody bothering to kill him."

Shadow sat back and sipped her ale thoughtfully.

"Now, that's odd," she said.

"Not really," Donya corrected. "Once some paltry thief becomes a public figure—"

"No," Shadow said slowly. "I mean this: What was this Pim fellow, a lousy low-rank thief, doing with a gold Guild token?"

"Pim couldn't have afforded a gold token on the best day of his life," Aubry argued. "Not unless he stumbled onto some luck I hadn't heard about. Cris?"

Cris toyed with the lamp wick.

"I thought he only had a copper token, same as me," he said absently. "I don't think he could have paid for more."

"Fortune curse his wealth," Shadow said impatiently. "What I mean is, why would Ganrom *let* him have a gold token, if he was that bad, and turn him loose in the Temple District to get caught and maybe spill all the Guild secrets he knew?"

Aubry raised his eyebrows.

"There isn't any 'let' to it, Shadow," he said mildly. "A thief can have whatever token he can afford, that's how Ganrom does it." He suddenly snatched the lamp out of Cris' hands and set it down firmly out of reach. "There!"

Shadow scowled, but said only, "A lot of good it did him, it seems. What happens to a thief's token when he dies?"

"That depends on who gets his hands on it," Aubry said. "He can keep it, or turn it in at the Guildhouse for half value. Or sell it to another thief for a few coppers under Guild price."

He glanced at Shadow eagerly.

"*Did* you get Pim's token?"

"I didn't say anything of the sort," Shadow said firmly. "And if I had such a thing—not that I have—I wouldn't sell it to anybody I liked, kinsman. Bet on it. A gold token doesn't seem to be a healthy thing to have around here."

"I suppose not," Aubry agreed reluctantly.

Donya gave Shadow a probing look.

"I think you know something I don't," she said.

"I know many things," Shadow said mysteriously. "Secret things. And if Aubry wants to come back to my room with me, I'll show him one or two of them. But only if he leaves the pipe. Come on, Aubry. I don't feel like having my brain picked tonight."

Aubry shrugged and grinned at Cris.

"Who can refuse an offer like that?" he said. "Cris, finish your ale and try not to burn the tavern down. Till later, Lady Donya."

Back at the Silver Dragon, Shadow peered out through a chink in her shutters.

"Aubry," she said, "do you have any idea who Ganrom might have following me?"

"Ha!" Aubry chuckled, making himself comfortable on Shadow's bed. "I don't. And if I did, I wouldn't be such a fool as to tell you and earn a knife in the back some dark evening. Why?"

"Because whoever it is, is Fortune-be-damned *good*," Shadow said exasperatedly. "I can't catch so much as a glimpse of him. Ganrom must be paying dearly. What bothers me is *why*, Fortune favor me, do I rate this kind of attention?"

Aubry shrugged.

"Maybe you should've tumbled Ganrom when he wanted it."

"Not unless someone sand-scoured him first." Shadow

grimaced. "If I wanted lice, fleas, and Fortune knows what else, there're pleasanter ways of getting them."

"Talk like that is probably what soured him," Aubry warned her. "How do you know I'm not going to walk out of this inn and right to Ganrom's door?"

"Because I'd carve you into thirty-three tiny pieces if you did." Shadow grinned. "And anyway, when I'm done with you tonight you won't be fit to walk."

She kicked her boots into a corner and pulled at the lacing on her tunic.

"That sounds like a challenge." Aubry smiled broadly.

Shadow chuckled and bolted the door securely.

"Bet on it," she said.

FOUR

Shadow yawned, stretched, and—*thunk!*—rolled out of bed onto the rough floor, the impact eliciting a yelp of pain which failed to awaken Aubry.

Rubbing her hip ruefully, Shadow groped for her wineskin and took a hearty swallow to rinse the morning sourness from her mouth. She opened the shutters and spat the mouthful out into the courtyard; a startled curse floated up in response.

Shadow closed the shutters again and slipped quietly into her clothes. Aubry was snoring loudly and drooling onto the pillow. Shadow chuckled quietly to herself, pocketed her gold, and tiptoed quietly out the door.

It was just past dawn, and the market was barely beginning to fill. Shadow stretched again, inserted the last pin into her coil of braids, and followed the enticing aromas of fresh cooking.

The morning was bright and warm, and Shadow was so in love with the day that she paid honestly for two fruit pastries, even though the vendor was conveniently busy popping the day's baking into his oven. Shadow mulled pleasantly over several possible plans for the day, then set out for Argent's shop. Argent and Elaria were just opening the store when she arrived.

"Good morn to you!" Argent smiled. "Did you get rid of your invisible companion?"

"For awhile." Shadow sighed. "Not that it was worth the trouble. Either the same person caught up with me later, or it was another one. Did you see anybody?"

Argent shook his head.

"No one came in," he said. "And there was no one out front, at least no one who appeared to be waiting for you to come out. I'm sorry."

"Not your fault." Shadow shook her head with reluctant admiration. "Whoever they've got tailing me is an expert, too good to be taken in so easily. I just can't imagine why I rate so much attention and expense. Professionals like that cost more Suns than I'd think Ganrom would waste on some transient, no matter how she ranks."

"What if it isn't Ganrom's hireling?" Argent suggested.

Shadow raised her eyebrows thoughtfully.

"Hadn't thought about it," she admitted. "But who in this town has reason to have me followed, besides Ganrom? And whoever it is has money and connections, too—hmmm."

"Idea?" Argent asked.

Shadow shook her head.

"I don't know," she said after a moment's thought. "I haven't crossed that many paths. There's the High Lord and Lady, of course, but anything they wanted to know about me they could've gotten easier and cheaper from Donya. There's that lord I robbed, but he doesn't know who I am—or shouldn't, at least. But—"

"But?" Argent prompted.

"But then there's that priest," Shadow said thoughtfully.

"The one we saw at the castle—Bobrick, that's the one. He gave me an odd look when I was in the Temple District yesterday, and I picked up my shadow after that. But why? If he's got that kind of connections, he'd have found out I'm not in High Lady Celene's pay."

"And even if you were, why should that bother him?" Argent added.

Shadow shrugged.

"This whole thing smells worse than my friend Aubry's pipe," she said with a grimace. "I'm beginning to wonder if a good rich market's worth the bother. It's getting so an honest thief can't walk the streets."

"You're not going to leave, are you?" Argent asked.

"Not yet." Shadow grinned. "This is beginning to get interesting."

"Then what will you do?" Elaria asked gently.

"Mmm. I need a look at that tail of mine," Shadow speculated, her eyes narrowing. "I think it's time to stir the pot and see what floats to the top."

Shadow found, to her delight, that the warrior Dalin still had a bit of dragon left to sell, and she didn't begrudge the five Moons she paid for a good-sized slab.

"Dalin," she said between bites, "I'm looking for Donya and I can't seem to find her. She said she was dining with some fellow named Derek, House of Batan, but she didn't say where. Do you have any idea?"

The tall, fair warrior thought it over for a minute.

"Derek? He's often found at the Gildensword, over in the Noble District," Dalin said at last. "Donya might have met him there. I can't imagine what she'd want with that hotheaded twit, anyway. He led a dragon hunt five months back and got three good warriors fair roasted, he did, charging the damned thing right in its lair."

"Maybe Donya wants to roast *him*." Shadow smiled.

"That's likely as not." Dalin snorted. "And Rhodon bless her if she does it."

The Gildensword, Shadow found, was frequented by young nobles with plenty of coin to wager over a throw of the dice; Shadow noted with interest that there was a noticeable lack of elvan patronage, unlike other similar institutions in Allanmere. As it wasn't a place where she could mingle inconspicuously, she wandered around near the front, planning her anticipated escape route and peeping in at the windows when she could.

Finally she spotted Derek at a table near the back. He was drinking and dicing with some other young nobles, and he appeared to be in high spirits. Shadow settled back to wait.

A brief prickling at the back of her neck reminded Shadow that she was still being watched; but try as she might, she could see no one who might be following her. She shook her head in admiration. A Fortune-blessed *good* professional. Her grin widened as she estimated the sum being spent by somebody to have her followed. Well, with but a touch from the right hand of Fortune, she'd know more shortly.

It was several hours before Derek finally took his leave of the Gildensword, staggering just a little. Shadow waited, peering around the corner of the building, until he was well into the street.

Quickly she darted forward, thrusting her foot between his boots. Derek flailed wildly for balance and lost, measuring his full length in the manure-spotted dust with a roar of drunken outrage. Shadow grabbed his purse and added a kick in the seat of the pants for good measure, paused briefly to give Derek a wave as he struggled to his feet, then dashed down the nearest alley with the young lord not far behind her.

Again Shadow could hear heavy footfalls and hoarse breathing drawing nearer behind her; but this time she wasn't worried. This was *her* chase, and Derek was playing his part beautifully.

Shadow dodged around another corner and confronted her chosen building, a ramshackle warehouse. She waited until Derek started to round the corner, touched the lock with her braceleted hand, and said loudly, "Aufrhyr." She had just time to duck through the door and slide the latch home before Derek crashed loudly into the wooden frame.

No time to spare. Shadow ·nimbly slipped out a dusty window and onto the roof, from which Derek could be seen battering at the flimsy door.

As Shadow had predicted, Derek eventually forced the aged latch, but after storming around the inside of the building for a few minutes, he came back out, cursing puzzledly. Shadow flattened herself on the roof, chuckling softly.

To Shadow's surprise, Derek headed directly for the Temple District, hardly looking about him as he hurried. Shadow, with her shorter stride, was hard-pressed to keep up and simultaneously avoid his infrequent backward glances; it was some time before she realized they were approaching the Temple of Urex.

Derek did not enter the temple, but rather snagged a messenger boy, handed him a Sun, and muttered a quick message in his ear. The boy nodded and disappeared into the temple. Derek waited outside, foot tapping impatiently against the temple steps.

In a few minutes the boy reappeared with a roll of parchment, which he handed to Derek.

Shadow scowled and edged closer under cover of a wagon, hoping for a look at the paper, but just as she glimpsed the penned characters Derek re-rolled the parchment, dismissed the messenger, and waited only a few moments before signaling yet another message-boy.

"Take this to Master Ganrom at the Guild of Thieves, and be quick about it," Derek ordered in a voice barely above a whisper, handing the boy the parchment and a Sun.

The messenger nodded, tucking the parchment into his belt, and trotted quickly south. Derek stood frowning for a moment, then headed back toward the Noble District.

Shadow cursed under her breath, her confusion almost as great as her frustration. What business had this lordling in the Temple of Urex, and with whom? And what business did either of them have with Ganrom?

"This is getting smellier than a ten-year outhouse," Shadow muttered darkly, torn between following the messenger or Derek. She chose the messenger.

Once out of Derek's sight, and with the gold already in his pocket, the boy slowed to a walk, occasionally pausing to peruse a booth or stall. When he stopped to buy sweets, Shadow saw her chance and carefully relieved him of the scroll.

The message was both cryptic and brief.

"She has discovered the power of the bracelet," it read. "Inform Blade to act immediately."

Shadow shook her head and deftly returned the scroll to the messenger's belt. She needed time to think, and the market was no place for that.

A quiet alleyway gave her a few moments' privacy, and she sipped wine from a skin thoughtfully. She needed another source of information. There was always Aubry to question, but if this involved the Guild, as it appeared, she couldn't be sure of his honesty. There was Argent, but his expertise seemed limited to the Mercantile District.

There was, of course, Donya—but was it really a good idea to get Donya involved in this? To Shadow's chagrin,

Donya often saw herself as a sort of rein on the elf's impetuous nature, as if she were an older sister rather than fifty-odd decades the younger. Shadow wanted neither a lecture nor a bodyguard. But still . . .

Shadow sighed resignedly and hurried toward the castle, sternly resisting the temptation to look behind her, although her instincts told her that she was, at least for the moment, rid of her follower.

To Shadow's relief, Donya was at home, and when the page reported Shadow's arrival, the warrior immediately came to greet her friend.

"What's the matter?" she asked, a worried frown creasing her brow. "For you to come here again, it must be big."

"Could be." Shadow shrugged. "Where can we talk privately?"

Donya raised her eyebrows.

"My rooms," she said. "This way."

Shadow had to chuckle when she saw Donya's suite which, in contrast to the opulence of the castle, was as stark and unluxurious as any humble warrior's. Donya ordered food and wine, received them, and left the maid with orders that they were not to be disturbed.

"Well, what is it?" Donya asked, watching Shadow attack the food. "Are you in trouble?"

Shadow shrugged again, her mouth full.

"Remains to be seen," she said after she swallowed. "Hopefully not *my* remains. Have you ever heard of someone named Blade before?"

"Oh, my."

Donya sat silent for a moment, then poured herself a mug of wine and refilled Shadow's goblet.

"Shady, are you sure you heard the name right?" she said soberly. "It couldn't have been another?"

Shadow nodded. "That bad, eh?" she asked.

"Not good," Donya admitted. "Blade's an assassin, Shady. One of the best—maybe *the* best. Nobody knows much about her or where she can be found; when you want to hire her, you just put out word and hope she's interested. Damned expensive, I hear, and persistent, too. It's said she followed Lord Davreen for six months and a hundred leagues before she finished him. Where in the world did you hear her name?"

"Call her the sauce on the pudding." Shadow grimaced. "Damn. No wonder I haven't been able to find out . . . damn."

"Find out what?" Donya pressed.

"Never mind," Shadow said firmly, shaking her head.

Donya sat back, frowning exasperatedly.

"Shady, don't you trust me after all this time?"

Shadow grinned halfheartedly.

"Friend," she said, "with my life I'd trust you, but with my secrets—well, since we're here in Allanmere, I'm not going to put too much strain on your loyalties. But tell me this: how much do you trust *me*?"

Donya was silent for a moment, tracing a finger around the mouth of her mug. Then she sighed and grinned back.

"With anything but my purse," she admitted. "Why?"

"Because I think I'm onto something big," Shadow said slowly. "At least, bigger than I thought at first. I'm not sure yet. I'll tell you everything as soon as I know more, but right now I'd rather not get you involved."

"Ah, Shady, Shady," Donya said sadly. "Always walking the thin edge of the sword."

"I think my balance is up to it." Shadow grinned.

"Just as long as you don't find Fortune's left hand wrapped around the hilt," Donya joked back, but the hurt showed in her eyes. "Well, you know best your own road, and no one else the wiser. And I know how useless it is to tell you to be careful. But watch sharp, friend, and remember that *no one* can claim my sword before you."

The seriousness in her friend's eyes made Shadow bite back a flip answer, and she squeezed Donya's calloused hand in her own smaller one.

"Now, that's a treasure that more than makes up for the family coffers." She smiled. "But listen, Doe. I'm going to be dropping out of sight for the next few days. I'm just telling you so you don't worry. I'm too visible to risk coming here, but if I need to, I'll leave word with Argent, all right?"

"Ah, Shady." Donya sighed and emptied her mug in a gulp. "You're sure there's nothing else I can do? Do you need money?"

"How noble do you think I am, now?" Shadow chuckled. "Don't wave the family gold under my nose; I might succumb. No, I'm fine, thanks."

"I guess that's it, then," Donya said reluctantly. "Come on, I'll take you out through one of the small gardens. If anyone followed you here, at least you should be able to slip past them leaving."

They followed a circuitous route, and Shadow was once more impressed with the size and complexity of the castle. A small corridor emerged into a beautifully laid out garden, from which Donya showed Shadow a cleverly concealed door opening into a clump of bushes on the riverbank north of the castle and outside the city walls.

"If you need to get in without being seen, remember this door," Donya told her. "It's a family secret, in case of battle; even the servants don't know about it." She gave Shadow a quick hug and hurried back through the garden.

As far as Shadow could tell, she had exited the castle unnoticed, and she was grateful for the respite. Instead of following the city wall east and reentering Allanmere through the North Gate, Shadow continued a little farther north, following the Brightwater northeast almost to the edge of the area of swamp known as the Dim Reaches, and then turning east into the forest. She needed time to think.

Shadow had left the Heartwood before the formal founding of Allanmere, but from what she understood of Allanmere's Compact with the forest elves, the treaty had been negotiated to limit the rights of humans over the forest, its land, game and timber. The forest had been divided into three concentric zones. In the Outer Zone, humans could hunt common game freely. In the Middle Zone, humans could travel and hunt only by special dispensation or under elvan escort. Humans were strictly forbidden to pass into the Inner Zone, however, except under very special circumstances and under strict supervision.

Shadow couldn't hope to reach the boundary of the Middle Zone in one day on foot, but it was a comforting feeling just to be in the forest again. She'd made no preparations and had only the few belongings she always carried—her tools, weapons, wine and gold—and that, she thought cheerfully, should be more than enough.

That comforting illusion did not persist for long.

Shadow sat brooding on a willow branch as the sun set, looking out over one of the many streams branching out from the Brightwater. It had been decades since she'd spent much time alone in the wilderness, and she'd grown used to entertainment and civilized comforts. She was bored, uncomfortable, and—surprisingly—lonely. Sighing, she went through the half-forgotten process of weaving the whiplike willow trailers into a hanging nest, then lay back with her wine and a hatful of berries.

She'd become complacent in her luck. Maybe she should've made a placating offer to Fortune's left hand! Now what did she have? A priest she didn't even know bearing her some grudge, a minor lordling who'd happily see her flayed, and a Guildmaster who wanted her dead! Not to mention one frighteningly efficient assassin on her trail, one who, for a change, probably could not be evaded simply by leaving Allanmere.

Remembering the last time she'd slept in this particular forest, Shadow had to chuckle to herself. She would never forget the lecture the tribal elder had given her the year she'd left the forest.

"Well, he was right." Shadow laughed. " 'Bored' *is* just a polite word for 'safe.' And it works in reverse, too, come to think of it!"

Then she sighed. Her tribe hadn't been any safer for their isolation.

"There's something to be said," she mused, "for spitting in safety's eye. At least it's an *amusing* way to get killed."

She pulled out one of the tabs of dreamweed resin, chewing it thoughtfully. All right, leaving was next to useless unless she could count on evading a reputedly skilled and *persistent* assassin for the rest of her life. Not a pleasant prospect to have hanging over her head. So what faced her in the city?

Blade.

"Buy her off?" Shadow murmured. "Ah, no. Really good professionals aren't bribable. Hurts their business. Kill her? Hah! Fortune favor you, Shady, and how vain are we feeling today? You haven't even been able to *see* her yet. What do you propose to do? Flip a dagger into the air and hope it lands on her head?"

Vikram, and his corpulent assistant, Bobrick.

"Now, there's a pair." Shadow grimaced, chasing the resin with a hearty gulp of wine and a handful of berries. "If a snake bit those two it'd die of the poison. But they don't seem willing to do anything themselves. Wonder why?"

Ganrom.

"Turtle turds," Shadow said disgustedly. "I probably should've tumbled the louse-ridden marsh puppy, then he might've left me alone. Now *there's* a pot of bitter ale—can't much appeal to my Guildmaster for help when he's the one who contracted my death! Hah! I'll see him squashed by Fortune's left hand if it costs me every copper I own, that six-fathered pisspot scraping who calls himself a Guildmaster."

Derek.

"He's the least of my worries," Shadow said wryly. "That crosseyed idiot couldn't walk and scratch his head at the same time. Still, he's a go-between. He could be useful later, I guess."

The bracelet.

"Somehow, this is the key to it," Shadow mused, gazing at the source of her woes. "Look at all the people who know about it—Vikram, Derek, Ganrom—hmmm. Have to add that mage Aliendra, I'll wager, and Argent, and Celene, too. Nobody to blame for those but myself. And Donya, yes, but she wouldn't talk. And Argent's got no reason to, nor Celene, unless she tells Sharl. Hmmm, Blade, can't forget her. Doubtless she knows more about the thing than I do."

Shadow's thoughts began to drift as the potent dreamweed resin worked its magic. She lit a pipe of leaf to help it along.

"Ah, Fortune, look at me." She sighed wistfully. "All I ever wanted was wine in my belly, the road under my feet, and fat merchants to rob. Is that so much to ask? Well, while I'm at it, a soft bed and a good tumble with a hearty fellow wouldn't be wasted on me, either. I'm an elf of humble needs, Lady Fortune. I don't deserve all these headaches."

Not at all to Shadow's surprise, it seemed that Fortune herself appeared on the willow branch not far away, seated comfortably on a floating cushion, her face, as always, veiled in darkness.

"Deserve? What in all the worlds has that to do with it?" Fortune snorted. She appeared not to notice that as the willow branch swayed, it passed through both the cushion and her lower body unimpeded. "If you want what you *deserve*, seek out that cult of monotheists who believe that after death they travel to paradise or perdition, depending on how virtuous a life they've led. I'm Fortune, child, the very essence of chance, and you want what you *deserve*?"

"Ah, no offense meant, Lady," Shadow said lazily. "On the whole I can't complain. It's been a good five hundred forty-two years so far."

"I should hope so," Fortune said impatiently. "You've had your share and more of My blessings, and even you, oh favored child, must occasionally feel the touch of My left hand. Do what you will with the luck I give you, be it good or ill. I bespeak the fall of the dice, but you alone place the bets. So don't groan to me, ungrateful elf child, for you'll wait long before I sculpt my whims to your liking. Either wait patiently for what comes to you, or go seek it on your own; but you'll get nothing lying in a tree and wishing for the gods to remake the world to suit you."

Abruptly the ill-defined form vanished from the branch.

"And right you are." Shadow sighed, unperturbed. "Ah, Argent, this *was* the good stuff." She yawned, stretched, and closed her eyes.

In the morning, Shadow abandoned her willow nest and the trade road and worked her way northeast, moving deeper into the forest at an easy lope. The Middle Zone was marked by a series of regularly placed stones engraved in glowing symbols, but Shadow passed them unconcernedly.

Shortly after she entered the Middle Zone, Shadow became aware of hidden eyes upon her. She ignored the feeling; this surveillance had nothing of the malign intent of her follower in the city.

It took nearly three days to cross the Middle Zone, and Shadow soon became impatient with her slow progress. A horse would have been worse than useless in the dense wood, and she was sure she was probably taking the most difficult way at that; her scant knowledge of the elvan patrol-trails was limited to the long ago and far away territories of her own people. In her youth, elves gifted with beast-speaking had often tamed and ridden the forest deer, and indeed Shadow saw many; but as she herself had no such gifts, she could only sigh wistfully and trot past.

The Inner Zone markers were placed more closely together, and shortly after she passed these, Shadow stumbled across a narrow but well-worn trail leading roughly in the right direction.

Shadow followed the track only as far as the nearest suitable campsite, although it was well before sunset when she stopped. There she laid a fire but did not light it, caught several fish at a nearby stream and cleaned them, and settled back to wait.

As she expected, she heard nothing even with her keen elvan ears; but near sunset she felt a familiar prickling at the back of her neck. Grinning, she lit her fire and laid out the fish.

"Join me and welcome, kinsfolk," she said. "I've food and fire, and lack only friends to share them."

The silence persisted so long that Shadow wondered if the traditional greeting had fallen out of use; but at last the bushes parted and three elves, two male and one female, stepped into the clearing, replacing arrows in quivers as they did so. All three were dressed in green tanned leathers.

The female and one of the males were as dark of hair and skin as Shadow, and nearly as short, but the second male was tall and fairer, with hair as red as autumn maple leaves.

"Welcome, Matriarch," the female said. "I'm Hawk, leader of this patrol; and my companions are Otter and Thorn. We are pleased to share your fire."

"I'm Nightshade." Shadow nodded. "Commonly known as Shadow, Shady to my friends."

"We've heard word of the Shadow-thief from our town kin," Thorn, the dark male, said with a smile. He sat down near the fire and skewered a piece of fish on a stick. "It's said the Guild has a new artist of some talent."

"Fortune's favored me so far," Shadow said modestly, accepting a proffered wineskin. "But the praise comes welcome from my kinfolk."

She filled her pipe with dreamweed and held out the pouch to Hawk, raising her eyebrows; Hawk accepted it with a nod of thanks.

"We of the Hidden Folk seldom leave the forest," she said slowly, sniffing the dreamweed critically and then smiling. "We depend on our traders to carry word back and forth. Strangers rarely visit us."

Shadow grinned at the veiled question.

"I'm not exactly a stranger," she said. "I was born to the Silverleaf tribe in Songwater. I doubt you've heard of them, though."

"My mother's half-sister was Silverleaf," Otter, the red-haired elf, said. "She and most of her kin were killed in the first raids of the Black Wars. We thought none survived, and Songwater has lain empty ever since."

Shadow shrugged, tilting a spitted fish over the fire.

"I got the road-itch and left the clan years before the wars," she said. "It was more than a century before I heard what had happened. It seemed useless to come back."

"Yet you are here," Hawk observed.

"I came to speak to the Eldest," Shadow said lightly. "And maybe visit the forest altars."

Thorn raised bushy eyebrows.

"Of those who leave the wood, few come back to the altars," he said curiously. "You have a gift for the wood sprite?"

" 'Wood sprite'?" Shadow grinned. "Is that what you call her now? We used to call her 'Greendaughter.' "

"Her?" Otter repeated. "You've seen it? None of the Hidden Folk knew if it were male or female—or something else altogether."

Shadow laughed this time.

"Oh, she'd enjoy that one! Yes, I've seen her. She's not an 'it', kinsman, and she's not a wood sprite, either," Shadow added. "Her name's Chyrie, and she's as elvan as you or I—more, probably."

Hawk narrowed earth-brown eyes framed in deep black lashes.

"You know this for fact?" she asked. "No one living today—except you—has seen the wood sprite. Sometimes our offerings are taken, more often not. Sometimes one of the folk, wounded in the forest, finds himself mysteriously transported to the boundaries of his clan, his wounds tended. Yet you give the spirit a name and call her one of us. She has spoken with you, then?"

Shadow shook her head, sipping her wine thoughtfully.

"I said I'd *seen* her," she corrected. "No, Chyrie never spoke to me. She never speaks. We had an . . . understanding, maybe. I suppose her story wasn't much known this side of the forest. Certainly it was common knowledge in Songwater, though, when I was young."

"Will you tell us this story?" Hawk asked eagerly. "And the Eldest, that it may be preserved?"

Shadow shrugged, refilling her pipe and cup.

"Why not?" she said. "I don't suppose it matters. Mind, it's just a tale passed down mother to child. I don't know it for full truth."

She settled back.

"How old is the Eldest?" she asked thoughtfully.

"He has almost nine centuries," Hawk told her.

"What I was told," Shadow said slowly, "is that Chyrie was born in the time your Eldest's grandfather would have first drawn breath."

"How could an elf live alone so long?" Otter protested.

Shadow shrugged.

"Maybe the Mother Forest keeps her, I don't know," she said. "Our Eldest used to say that Chyrie had forgotten her mortality."

"The wood sprite has been there for as long as any remember," Thorn said thoughtfully. "But if she is kin, why remain apart?"

"Chyrie was born not far from Songwater," Shadow said. "There were tribes there even more isolated than the Silverleaf clan, tribes who had never been seen even by other elves. The clans were different then, inbred and hostile and territorial, and some of them had odd customs among themselves. Chyrie was born to a tiny band who called themselves Wildings and left it at that. They were, too—wild, I mean. Most of the clan wandered through their territory singly or in mated pairs, sleeping here or there, hunting and watching the borders. Touchy about them, too!

"Anyway, this was in the time when the very first humans had come to farm the southwest edge, where Allanmere is now. The way I hear it, Chyrie was raped by some barbarians on the leading edge of an army coming down from the north. They come in waves every few centuries, you know—that wave wasn't the first, and the Black Wars probably won't be the last.

"Well, Chyrie. For some reason she and her mate befriended some humans—some of the more civilized ones, that is—and traveled with them through the forest, uniting the tribes against the barbarian army. It's said she fought alongside the humans herself, I don't know. I know her mate was killed, though, and Chyrie survived to bear the fruit of her rape—a human son and an elvan daughter. She left the daughter with the humans and the son with the elves, and vanished into the forest with her mate's body. The elvan unity fell apart not long after that, and there weren't enough humans left to finish the town. Chyrie's daughter Ria wed the son of the town's lord later—that was Sharl II—and they returned to rebuild the town, not long before the Black Wars. Ria's relationship with Chyrie and the forest tribes enabled her and Sharl II to form the Compact with the elves and complete the walls of Allanmere before the Black Wars began. Anyway, nobody heard much of Chyrie after Ria's birth."

"But Sharl II and Ria never bore an heir," Thorn said curiously. "A human named Valann, supposedly a relative, took an elvan wife and assumed the throne of Allanmere."

"Uh-huh." Shadow nodded. "But he wasn't Sharl II's relative; he was Ria's. Her brother, to be exact, raised in the Heartwood and already mated with an elvan wife who was fortunately fertile. It was their son, Sharl III, who founded the ruling line of Allanmere."

"But why did Chyrie—?" Otter began, but Shadow only shrugged.

"Who knows how she thinks?" Shadow said. "Maybe she's forgotten she's one of us. She lives in the forest like a beast, but she's never quite left us. As you know, she visits the altars and takes what she wants. Occasionally she gives her help in one form or another. My thought is, she's made her choice and she's happy where she is. Some don't agree, but they've never found her, either."

"Yet you found her," Hawk said skeptically.

"I should say *she* found *me*." Shadow grinned ruefully. "She's a beast-speaker, you know, and Fortune alone knows what other of the old gifts she has. Some used to say she could hear our minds speak. If so, no wonder she stays where she is!

"I met Chyrie not long before I left the forest. I was a wanderer," Shadow remembered with a smile. "Always off on my own, and young enough to be rash about it, too. Never mind about clan boundaries or patrols! I'd go on month-long treks through the outer woods, skirting the edges to watch those fascinating humans at their farms or as they traveled by. But as the humans moved in, they found the forest handy for poaching—as you know—and they left their traps for unwary animals and unwary elves, too. And that's what happened to me; I stumbled right into a pit, and there I was.

"I waited for days, hoping a human would come and fearing one would; but I guess the pit had been dug and then forgotten, or the human killed by the patrols. I couldn't climb out, and nobody knew where I was, and the little water from the dew wasn't enough. I was cold, and hungry, and desperately thirsty, and before long I was only a half-dead husk of an elf, mostly skin and bone." Shadow shook her head. "I was sure I'd never see another sunrise when I closed my eyes, and the way I felt, I didn't much care.

"When I woke, though—half-woke, really—I was being jolted about, slung over somebody's shoulder like a sack of tubers and carried off. I was too weak to fight, but I wasn't too weak to think, and think I did. I imagined it was some

human, come to claim his prey, and Fortune alone knew
what he'd do with me! There wasn't much to be done,
though, but play dead and hope I'd have a chance to do
something later; so I closed my eyes and played dead.
Wasn't hard, I was close enough in truth, anyway. I faded
in and out and in and out until I thumped down on some
surface, and then there was water in my mouth."

Shadow shook her head at the memory and took a healthy
swig of her wine.

"Friends, I'll tell you here and now that no wine ever
tasted as wonderful as that water, and a lake of it wouldn't
have been too much. But I got only a sip, just enough to wet
my lips, and later a little more, a sip at a time. Then I sensed
whoever it was leaving, although they were elvishly quiet
about it, and I opened my eyes.

"I was in a cave, or rather, a burrow. It was small and
dim and close, barely big enough to stand up in, and you
couldn't have taken two steps. I was lying on a big bundle
of furs, there was another bundle of stuff in a niche in the
wall, a bark lamp beside me on the floor, a few containers
and such crammed in at one side, and that was all. There
was a tunnel leading slantwise up, and I could see daylight
through it. Then the daylight darkened, and I closed my
eyes and lay back again.

"My rescuer put something down on the floor and raised
my head, and some sort of paste was put in my mouth. It
tasted like some sort of potion—a sleep-potion, probably—
and I pretended to swallow it, but hid the stuff in my cheek
until whoever it was left again. Then I spit the potion out
and buried it, and lay back again and watched through my
lashes.

"By that time, I had the idea that it wasn't any human
who had me there." Shadow grinned. "But I'd scarcely

expected Chyrie Greendaughter herself. That's who it was, though, and I knew it as soon as I saw her.

"She was dressed in leathers like any of the woodfolk," Shadow remembered, "but the leathers were stained as green as yours, and odd bits fastened here and there like leaves or bits of bark. You couldn't have seen her in a thicket unless she screamed at you. Her hair was tawny instead of black, chopped off short, and her eyes were the color of amber and slit-pupilled like a cat's—some of those hidden tribes used to look really odd, you know. She was very small, almost as small as me."

Shadow paused to refill her pipe and mug before she resumed her story.

"The most amazing thing was her skin, though. Everywhere it showed it was covered with the most amazing pictures. Yes, pictures, like you'd paint on a hide, but these were on *her* hide. Her whole skin was covered with the design of a vine. You could almost smell the flowers. I've never seen anything like it, before or since.

"My sleeping act must have fooled her. She fed me some stew and left me be. After sunset she brought me more of the potion, and I spit it out after she was gone. I slept anyway; I was that worn out. In the morning, though, she came with some more, and I figured I'd take a chance.

"I just opened my eyes and said, 'There's no need for that, and I'd just as soon feed myself for breakfast.' "

"What did she do?" Thorn asked eagerly.

"She sat back on her heels and stared at me for quite awhile with those odd eyes." Shadow grinned. "Then she half-smiled and handed me a bowl of porridge and a cup of water, and watched while I finished them.

"It took me two days to get fit to go home," Shadow remembered. "And Chyrie just sat and watched me, helped me outside when I needed it, and brought food and water.

When I was well enough, she led me to the boundaries of Silverleaf lands—mind you, I'd never *said* I was Silverleaf—and left me there."

"But you saw where she lived," Hawk pressed.

Shadow smiled, staring into the fire.

"Yes," she said. "I saw her den."

"And you never went back?" Otter asked disappointedly.

"I never went near her den again. And I never told anyone where it was," Shadow said firmly. "Small enough repayment, I guess. Not that it matters much, I suppose—a wily thing like Chyrie would've moved it anyway, or had more than one. And that's my tale, such as it is."

"And you return now," Hawk said, giving Shadow a probing look.

"As I said, I want to speak to the Eldest." Shadow shrugged. "I've fallen out of touch with the forest. And I'll visit the altars and leave something, yes. But it's pointless sending someone to follow me in hope of getting a glance at Chyrie. I doubt she'd come out; she's probably long forgotten me. And anyway, you can be sure she'd know of any watchers, no matter how good they were, or you'd have seen her before now."

Hawk said nothing, but frowned disappointedly.

"Anyway, why so many questions?" Shadow said after a moment. "Granted, it's been centuries since I set foot in the Heartwood, but I've never met any elves anywhere so concerned with a kinswoman's personal business. Has the welcome grown less since I left, or privacy grown less valued?" She smiled to soften the rebuke.

Thorn nodded embarrassedly.

"We hear little news here from the town," he said. "As Hawk said, it's rare that strangers visit us—or even kin who have left the forest. Perhaps we see significance where there is none. But no discourtesy is meant, Matriarch."

"Shady," Shadow corrected.

"Shady." Thorn grinned.

"So how much further do I have to go?" Shadow asked. "I didn't think it'd take this long when I left, but I've gotten soft over the centuries."

"At your pace, you'd run a day and half more," Hawk told her. "But Otter can take you back, as his time on wide patrol is almost done."

"Since when does an elf need an escort in the Inner Zone?" Shadow asked, frowning.

"You need no escort," Hawk said placidly, "but you may want a mount. Otter is a beast-speaker, and the stag he rides home can bear you also."

"Now, that's a welcome offer," Shadow admitted, "and one I'll accept with my heartfelt—or footfelt—thanks." She reached for the pipe.

Thorn took a last puff, his eyes sparkling, and handed it over.

"Is that the only offer you're likely to accept?" he asked slyly.

Shadow took a long puff of the potent dreamweed, then drained her mug of wine.

"It's the only offer I've been made, so far," she said lazily, cocking one eyebrow. "Are you going to change that?"

"Some of our ancient traditions still remain," Thorn teased. "It would still be considered rude to let our visiting kinswoman sleep cold and lonely in her pallet."

"Well, I'm glad to hear that that custom hasn't changed." Shadow chuckled. "But you make it sound suspiciously like a polite favor to an aging Matriarch."

"I meant no such thing," Thorn protested with a grin. "But if you must consider it a favor, think of it as the sophisticated Matriarch consenting to pass on some of her expertise to a rather inexperienced but enthusiastic young fellow."

Shadow threw back her head and laughed until the tears ran from the corners of her dark eyes.

"If you put it like that," she gasped, "how can I refuse?"

FIVE

"My, how things have changed," Shadow murmured, craning her neck while she clutched at Otter's belt for balance. The stag's back was broad enough, but the spine made an uncomfortable ridge. "The central village was in Inner Heart when I left, and this is right in the middle of what used to be Moon Lake lands."

"A large part of Inner Heart burned during the wars," Otter told her. "Afterwards, the village was so large that it was moved to the edge of Moon Lake to provide fish and water for so many, since much of the game had been driven away by the fighting. There—you can see it now."

Shadow's eyes widened, but she said nothing, inwardly marveling at the sight.

Moon Lake was much the same as ever, large and clear and still; but now the west edge was a cluster of huts, both on the ground and suspended from the huge old trees, and numerous boats were drawn up on the mossy shores. Shadow could see more than fifty of the huts, and elves were everywhere, fishing from the shore or from boats, preparing meat or skins or fish, or just sitting about and talking.

The village was, of course, tiny compared to the bustling labyrinth of Allanmere, but Shadow had never seen so many elves in one place at a time. She smiled to see the small packs of children running about as wild and heedless as ever—that much had not changed.

The stag was growing restive, so Otter stopped at the outskirts of the village and helped Shadow down. She winced, rubbing her tailbone, and thought that walking, perhaps, was not so bad after all.

"The Eldest will doubtless be in his lapidary this time of day," Otter told her. "He's a fine hand at it and makes a pretty trade. Will you see him there, or wait until the evening fire?"

"I'll go now, I think," Shadow said with a rueful sigh. "The Heartwood may have been my home, but it's been so long that I feel a bit like a troll out of his hole, wandering about."

The lapidary was a small but centrally located hut, presently occupied by a single elf, his braid of fire-red hair coiled neatly at the back of his head, polishing a faceted topaz. He looked up as they entered, then smiled.

"Eldest, this is Shadow—ah, Nightshade, once of the Silverleafs," Otter said. "Shady, our Eldest, Aspen."

"Welcome, kinswoman." Aspen started to extend his hand, which was covered with polishing grit, then looked down at it and grinned sheepishly. "Your pardon. Sit, if you can find a clean spot."

"My pleasure, Grandfather." Shadow found a tipped-over section of log in a corner and rolled it over. "Please, go on with what you were doing."

Aspen nodded his acknowledgment and resumed polishing thoughtfully.

"Nightshade, eh, of the Silverleaf clan?" he mused. "Not the Wandering Child?"

"The same." Shadow laughed. "I didn't know I was that notorious."

"There were few clans on whose territories you failed to trespass, at one turn of the seasons or another." Aspen smiled. "I had forty decades when you were born, and forest news travels to Inner Heart if nowhere else. But you left before the wars, true?"

Shadow nodded.

"I've been chasing the ends of the road since then," she said with a sigh. "Sometimes it's easier to stay away and remember your home as you left it, than to return and see how much it's changed. But I found myself not far away with empty pockets, and decided to see if Allanmere's market was all I'd heard. What a city Allanmere's become! Hard to believe one little stone-walled half-village could have grown into such a monster!"

"The changes seem less, when seen over the course of the decades," Aspen admitted. "And we of the Hidden Folk see little change at all. Is this only a visit, or will you take a place in the town or here?"

"Just a visit." Shadow hesitated. "Have you heard anything of the Guild in Allanmere?"

Aspen shook his head. "Little since Evanor was killed. The Guild was largely our voice in Allanmere until that time—few elves have the inclination to sit on Council, and even fewer pay much attention when they do. Since Evanor died and elves in the Guild became few, we in the forest have largely left the Guild and the city to itself."

"A pity." Shadow pushed up her sleeve and removed the bracelet, holding it out for Aspen's inspection. "Have you ever seen anything like this? Do you know anything about it?"

Aspen raised one red eyebrow, then put down the topaz, wiped his hands, and took the bracelet. He inspected it closely for some moments without a word, then handed it back to Shadow.

"Indeed I know it," he said slowly. "I myself cut the gems for this magical toy and shaped its metal. See, here is my mark. It belonged to Evanor. If I may ask, kinswoman, how came you by it?"

"In a way Evanor would've approved." Shadow shrugged. "I liberated it from a young noble in the market. The trouble is, there seem to be a number of people in town who know what the thing is and want it. I don't know how that noble came by it or how so many people are involved with it, but I'd be interested in finding out."

"As would I." Aspen's brown furrowed. "As best I would know, Evanor kept it by him always, but it was not on his body when it was returned to the forest. His left hand, however, had been severed."

Shadow frowned.

"Would it work for anyone, human or elf?" she asked.

"If they knew the word to summon its power." Aspen nodded. "Therefore, if his hand was severed to remove it, the one who robbed his body could not have known how to use it. Indeed, beyond Evanor and myself, I know none who would have known it as other than ornament."

"What about the mage who bespelled it?" Shadow asked.

"None. Evanor brought forth its enchantment himself," Aspen told her. "He had twelve centuries and a decade or two at his death, and was well versed in the old magics."

Shadow's eyebrows shot up.

"I didn't know he was a mage, or so old," she said, shaking her head. "Who would've killed him—and who *could* have?"

"No one is beyond the skill of some assassins." Aspen

shrugged. "It's long known that the human Ganrom hired it done to gain the Guild seat."

"Must've been some Fortune-blessed *good* assassin," Shadow muttered darkly. "Listen, how long would it take to have another bracelet made, identical to this one in appearance?"

Aspen thought for a moment.

"It is fine work, but not difficult," he mused. "Perhaps five days, with the aid of my apprentices. You think to bait those who took the bracelet?"

"Something like that. This is getting as twisted as a pricklevine," Shadow said ruefully. "But I'll pay you well for the copy, in gold and in a story I know you'll want to hear."

"A story?" Aspen prompted.

"The tale of your wood sprite." Shadow grinned. "Interested?"

Aspen's eyes widened, and he put away his polishing tools.

"Come to my hut," he said. "There is wine and food, and I will most eagerly hear your tale."

"How wonderful," Aspen said when she finished, shaking his head. "I had heard mention of the Wilding clan, but they were gone long before the Black Wars—perhaps during the first incursions in this area—and were never seen by other tribes even when they flourished in their own places. It seems incredible."

"I don't blame you if you don't believe me." Shadow shrugged. "It's a pretty fantastic tale, I'll grant you that."

"I believe," Aspen reassured her, refilling her mug with wine. "You mentioned the pictures on her skin, the flowering vine. Skin art is a very ancient talent, practiced in only a few tribes and by only a few very specially gifted artists.

Doubtless this Chyrie, or her mate perhaps, was one such. That art has almost died out among us. It involved using special dyes and pricking designs into the skin with a needle."

Shadow grimaced at the thought.

"Ugh," she said. "That's a lot of nastiness for a little decoration. Reminds me of a backwards human lot to the west, who cut themselves up to make decorative patterns of scars all over their faces and arms. But, speaking of arm—what will you take for the bracelet? To have it ready as soon as you can, and maybe send it by way of somebody coming to town?"

Aspen sat silent for a moment, thoughtfully swirling the wine in his cup.

"Evanor was friend and kin," he said at last. "Let it be thus—if you bring the one responsible for his death to the elves for judgment and punishment at our hands, or see to it yourself, I will charge you nothing. If you cannot do so, a thousand Suns or the bracelet returned to us for sale."

Shadow nodded.

"More than fair," she said. "I won't even haggle that price. But truth be told, Grandfather—"

"Aspen, please."

"Aspen," Shadow agreed. "Truth to tell, I'm not so much concerned with Evanor as I am with Shady. Forgive me, but Evanor's dead and gone and beyond enjoying his revenge, and I'm more worried about seeing that I don't follow him back to the Mother Forest. I'm mainly concerned with finding out who's put a top-notch assassin on *my* trail."

Aspen looked at her inquiringly.

"You might be able to help me, at that," Shadow said suddenly. "With your friendship with Evanor—did you ever hear anything about a professional named Blade?"

Aspen's head jerked up as though he had been struck, and his eyes widened.

"You are certain that is the one?" he said, his voice tight. "You could not be mistaken?"

"I'd wager my last skin of wine on it," Shadow said drily. "Well, go on—I knew it was bad, but I didn't know it was *that* bad."

"Evanor knew of this Blade," Aspen said slowly. "She was one of very few professional killers skillful enough to have killed Evanor. But of course, Evanor's left hand was gone, which is much unlike her style."

"Professionals almost never take anything off the body." Shadow nodded. "But you say Evanor knew her? Is she an elf?"

"No!" Aspen paused. "Evanor said she was no elf. Yet she has worked her trade for more years than accountable for a human's short life. Evanor had some quiet dealings with her upon occasion, for she is reliable and works independently, not with the Aconite Circle."

"Oh?" Shadow raised her eyebrows. "That's curious. Can you tell me anything else about her: what she looks like, how she kills?"

Aspen shook his head.

"I know nothing more than hearsay, beyond what I have told you," he said regretfully. "Her appearance none can tell. Her methods are varied, but most often she kills with the knife. In some cases I might suspect poison, for her victims were sometimes found dead with but insignificant wounds. Otherwise I know only that she is formidable; indeed, it is said that she has never failed a contract."

"Delightful." Shadow sighed. "It looks like Fortune's left hand is giving me a good whack this time to make up for past negligence. Any advice?"

"I doubt Blade would dare the Inner Zone," Aspen suggested. "You would be safe enough here."

"What, and wait for her to die of old age?" Shadow laughed ruefully. "From what you say, it might be a long wait! This is a full chamberpot slopping over, bet on it. Hmmm, what about hiring another expert to take her out?"

"One of the Circle might be induced to do so, as she operates outside their influence," Aspen said doubtfully. "But such a one need be either very skilled or very foolish."

"Foolish as an elf who gets involved in things that are none of her affair," Shadow agreed with a grin.

"There is that," Aspen admitted. "But is there nothing else I can do to help?"

"Don't think so." Shadow sighed. "I need to start back to Allanmere right away. I'd like to borrow a mount, though, if that's possible, and buy a few odds and ends, and visit the altars."

"Of course." Aspen's smile was warm. "I hope your next visit need not be so hasty."

"I hope I'll be alive to *make* the next visit." Shadow laughed. "Have your messenger leave the bracelet with Lady Donya—that shouldn't arouse suspicion—and I'll leave a thousand Suns with her, just in case."

Shadow did not linger at the village, but purchased a little food and wine, some plain but sturdy garment leather and sewing needs, a comb, some metal fishing hooks and—after a moment's thought—a vial of moly extract. Some of the food and wine went into her pack with the vial, and she loaded the rest in a sack onto the doe awaiting her at the edge of the clearing.

It was nearing evening when she reached the first of the forest altars. The carven stone blocks were scattered over a wide area, each in its own particular clearing. Most held some offering or another—trinkets, coin, even valuable jewelry—but Shadow ignored them, following the winding paths until she reached an isolated and empty altar.

Shadow emptied the bag and spread its contents on the altar, took a skin of wine and a cake from her pack, and sat down to wait.

The shadows lengthened, the sunlight filtering down through the leaves grew dim. The cake was long gone, its crumbs donated to feed the squirrels; the wineskin lay flaccid and abandoned on the ground. The doe had long since wandered away. Shadow dozed.

She came awake instantly, the back of her neck prickling. There was no sound beyond the ordinary noises of the forest, but there was the unmistakable sensation of eyes upon her. Shadow sat back against the tree trunk, watching the altar and waiting.

There was no moment of transition. One moment the clearing around the altar was empty; the next moment there was a small brown figure beside the stone, the twining of bright green "leaves" about its tanned skin making it all but invisible against the bushes. One wiry brown hand reached out to touch the leathers and comb; the slanting amber eyes fixed unblinkingly on Shadow's.

"No criticism intended." Shadow grinned. "You look fine as you are."

The amber eyes turned briefly to the altar again. The elf held up one of the fishhooks, then turned back to Shadow and gave a quick half-smile.

"They think you're a wood sprite." Shadow chuckled. "The embodiment of the Mother Forest. I doubted if anybody would bother leaving anything practical for a forest spirit. Jewels and trinkets, that's all I've seen. If you—"

Something in the slit-pupiled eyes silenced her, making her words seem irrelevant. Chyrie lifted the wineskin from the altar and stepped closer. She uncorked the skin and drank, then passed the skin to Shadow, eyes expectant.

Shadow took a swallow from the skin and handed it back.

Chyrie stoppered the wineskin and put it, with the other contents of the altar, back into the leather sack. She withdrew something from a clump of bushes at the edge of the clearing and walked back to press it into Shadow's hand: a small leather pouch.

"Thank you," Shadow said, surprised. "But you didn't need to—"

A calloused brown finger touched her lips, silencing her. The amber eyes smiled into hers, and the small hand briefly touched her cheek. Then the clearing was empty again, the altar bare. At one edge of the clearing, however, was a stag, waiting patiently beside Shadow's pack.

Shadow shivered, then smiled.

"Thank you," she whispered, unnecessarily.

After a moment she opened the small leather pouch and looked inside. There was a small bone flask in the pouch, intricately carved with the same vine design Chyrie wore on her skin. Carefully, Shadow worked the stopper out of the flask and sniffed at the opening; the aroma was delicious but unfamiliar. Shadow put the stopper back. She tucked the pouch into the front of her tunic and loaded her pack onto the stag, climbing on herself with the aid of a stump.

Riding, it took only two days to reach the outer edge of the forest; each morning when Shadow awakened, the stag would be there waiting. It did not leave until noon of the third day, when Shadow glimpsed Allanmere through the thin veil of the forest's edge. Shadow sent it on its way with an affectionate grin, shouldered her pack, sighed happily, and set her feet on the road.

Shadow debated several possible courses, then settled on sneaking into the city in a farmer's wagon. She made her way cautiously to Argent's shop, avoiding the main roads, and used the bracelet to enter the store by way of the back door.

Argent was out front, dealing with a customer by the sound of it. Shadow sat down at his desk, putting her feet up, and lit a pipe of dreamweed while she waited.

After a few minutes the bargain ended (Shadow grinned; she could've talked Argent down another ten Moons), and Argent came back, sniffing the air puzzledly. He started violently when he saw Shadow.

"By leaf and tree, do you drop out of the air now?" He chuckled weakly.

"No, I just sneak in by the back door." Shadow laughed. "I hope you don't mind just this once."

"Not at all." He gazed rather sternly, however, at Shadow's feet on his desk; Shadow grinned innocently, but took them down.

"But where have you *been*?" Argent continued. "I've been looking for you for days, and Donya's been here a dozen times if once."

"Oh?" Shadow raised an eyebrow. "I told her I'd be gone. Has anything new happened?"

"Anything new?" Argent exclaimed. "The city's on the brink of disaster and she innocently asks—"

"Well, don't make me beg." Shadow sighed. "Let's have it."

"The Council of Churches is in an uproar, to begin with," Argent told her. "The very night after you left, the Temple of Urex was burglarized. High Priest Vikram's assistant, Bobrick, was beaten near to death and two novices were killed, and the most valuable relics were stolen."

"Did anybody see anything?" Shadow asked.

"No, only Bobrick and the novices were in the temple then, and Bobrick was struck unconscious from behind.

Vikram believes the thieves got in and escaped through the dungeon grating at the rear."

"Well, what then? It's still up in the air?"

"The Temple of Argron caught a couple of scruffy fellows robbing the offering urns." Argent shrugged. "As far as I know there's nothing to link them with the robbery at the Temple of Urex, but Vikram saw it differently. He petitioned the City Council for permission to have them put to death. The Guild started screaming about that, and the petition was refused, so Vikram had their hands struck off and hamstrung them—"

"Nasty." Shadow winced.

"That's but the beginning," Argent said. "Two days later the High Priest of the Temple of Argron was found on Guild Row, hung up by his heels and his throat slit. Vikram announced that any known thief found in the Temple District would have his hands and feet cut off and his eyes put out. High Lord Sharl would have none of that, and there's a pretty debate raging on now between the Council of Churches and the Guild, with the City Council caught in the middle."

"Ouch." Shadow puffed meditatively on her pipe for a moment. "On a more personal front, any better news?"

"Perhaps." Argent hesitated. "The day after you left, two elves came into the shop asking about you. One was fair-haired, rather stocky for an elf, and the other was—"

"Shorter, light brown hair, green eyes, stinking pipe?" Shadow guessed.

"Yes. You know them?"

"More or less." Shadow frowned. "But they shouldn't know about *you*. I'd swear by Fortune's tits that I never mentioned your name to him. Was there anyone else in the shop when they came, or while they were here?"

Argent's forehead creased as he thought.

"My attention was on the elves," he admitted. "But it seems to me that perhaps there was someone else who came in, either before they did or while we were talking. Elaria would know; she has an eye for faces. I'll get her."

Argent left, closing the door behind him, and after a wait that left Shadow rather impatient, reappeared with his sister.

"Sorry," he said. "I had to close the shop. Lara, wasn't there someone else here when those two elves came in the other day? A woman, wasn't it?"

Elaria thought for a moment, then nodded.

"A human woman, young," she said. "She came in just before them and left just after. She bought nothing but a little moonflower tea and some spices."

"Can you remember what she looked like?" Shadow asked eagerly.

"Hmmm." Elaria frowned. "Do you know, it's the oddest thing, but I never really seemed to be able to get a good look at her. She had dark hair, I remember, cut short. Black, maybe. Pale skin. She was dressed in black, I know that much, even gloves. Tall for a human woman, perhaps a little taller than Lady Donya."

She thought a moment longer, then shook her head regretfully.

"I'm sorry," she said. "That's all I remember."

"What about her voice?" Shadow asked.

"I never heard it," Elaria said. "She merely handed me a list."

Shadow jolted upright in her chair. "Have you still got it?"

"Why, yes. Argent and I were so concerned with the elves coming in that I just tossed it under the counter when she left," Elaria said excitedly. "Wait, I'll get it."

Elaria returned with a scrap of plain paper and handed it to Shadow. Shadow scanned the list, then nodded.

"This wasn't scribed," she said with a sigh of relief. "The handwriting's too ordinary, and there's no scribal seal. There's a good chance she wrote it herself."

"That isn't very common, though, is it?" Argent asked, curious. "Most folk who can't afford a scribe can't write, either."

"No. But there's two choices here," Shadow reminded him. "Either this woman's got nothing to do with me at all, in which case it doesn't matter, or she *does*. And if she does, she wouldn't want to draw attention to herself by bribing a non-scribe to write a common shop list, when she could obviously just ask for the things she wants. But she wouldn't speak, because speaking would draw the listener's gaze to her face, and voices can be memorable. And she wouldn't use a scribe, because then anyone could trace her back to that scribe by the seal."

"But what good do you think the note will do you?" Elaria asked practically. "It wouldn't hold enough of an impression for a good divination, would it?"

"No, it wouldn't." Shadow grinned. "But I've got an idea it'll serve another purpose. She may be damned good, and experienced, too, but I think she's made a slipup here. Listen, Argent, I'm going to sneak out the back again. I'll get back to you this evening, if I can. I'm going to have to find somewhere less public than the Silver Dragon to stay."

"You're welcome to stay at my house," Argent offered. "It's secluded enough, and safer than an inn."

"Argent, are you sure you should become involved in this?" Elaria asked gently.

"It appears that I'm already involved." Argent shrugged. "The Guild, at least, now associates Shadow with our shop. If she stays with me, at least she needn't come here again, and that would be safer for her and us as well. Shadow?"

Shadow raised her eyebrows thoughtfully.

"It's an idea," she admitted. "Of all the places people might look for me, I doubt if the Noble District will be high on their list. Thank you, Argent, and I'll meet you there tonight."

Shadow skirted the market and located Uncle in the dusty plaza where she'd first found him. As usual, there were half a dozen urchins in attendance, and Shadow called them around.

"I'm looking for a fellow," she said, and described Aubry to them. "This Moon goes to the first one of you who finds him for me—without anyone knowing you're looking! Check the Three-Spangled Horn and the Guildhouse first. When you find him, tell him that Shady wants to talk to him, and bring him here *without* saying where you're going. Got it?"

The ragged children scampered off with gratifying haste, and Shadow sat down beside Uncle and popped a Sun into his cup.

"Strange doings these days, lady elf," Uncle said, cackling. The Sun vanished mysteriously into his rags. "You'll pardon me for saying, but I may be risking these old bones just being seen with the likes of you."

"I'll pardon you, and you're right." Shadow grinned. "I'll only trouble you long enough to offer you ten Suns to answer a question for me, and then forget I asked it."

"And if I don't know the answer?"

"Then I'll give you five Suns anyway, just to let your memory slip," Shadow told him. "Deal?"

"Aye."

"How do I find a Fortune-be-damned *good* member of the Aconite Circle who might be willing to take on a chancy job?"

Uncle's single eye widened.

"Oho! A strong move, Matriarch! But if the job's the one I'm thinking of, you'll not find a one."

"It's not the one you're thinking of—exactly," Shadow told him. "Nobody that good would be that stupid. Can you help me?"

"Aye," Uncle said curiously. "But the fellow you'd be best asking is your own Guildmaster. From what I hear, he could set it up cheaper."

"Trust me, he's one person I *can't* ask," Shadow said ruefully. "So what can you tell me?"

"There's a place on Guild Row called the Black Lotus," Uncle told her. "Go there and ask the barkeep for Dragon's Blood. He'll ask you what year, and you tell him you want the same vintage that Tigan drinks. Convince him and he'll set you up—for the right price, of course."

"Of course." Shadow counted out the Suns and handed them to Uncle. "One more thing."

"Eh?"

"I know how things work in the marketplace," Shadow told him. "I don't have any illusions about loyalty. But if somebody starts asking about me, I want a chance to top their offer."

Uncle threw his head back and wheezed with laughter.

"Aye, Matriarch," he gasped. "That I'll grant you for the asking."

"Then maybe I can buy a little more information," Shadow said thoughtfully. "I'm going to be needing money, and a lot of it. Here's what I want . . . "

They talked in whispers until Tig materialized beside them.

"Mevan's bringing him, lady," he panted to Shadow. "He'll be here in a minute or two."

"Thanks for the warning, Tig, that was sharp," Shadow told him, handing him a copper. She folded her arms, surreptitiously checking the placement of a concealed dagger, and waited.

Tig needn't have bothered; the odor of Aubry's pipe announced his presence moments before the elf trotted into the plaza behind the young girl. He slid to a stop when he saw Shadow, a grin lighting his face.

"Shady! By the altars, I only half-believed this scamp when she said you asked for me. I've been chasing about the town—"

"So I hear," Shadow said mildly. She tossed the Moon to Mevan. "And why have you been in such a race to find me?"

"Why, you just vanished on me," Aubry protested. "I woke up at the inn and you were gone, and no word of you on the street. Things as they were, I was afraid—well, you know." He glanced at Uncle.

Shadow nodded and motioned Aubry to a quiet corner.

"Mmmm. But what made you think of looking for me at the herbal shop?" Shadow pressed.

"Why, I got a note," Aubry said blankly. "It said that if I wanted news of you, to ask there. I thought maybe you'd sent it, being careful. I hoped so, anyway. But the fellow there wouldn't tell me a thing. Then I thought maybe it was a trick, and I've been checking around ever since."

"Did you keep the note?" Shadow asked, thawing a little.

"You think I'm a fool?" Aubry rummaged in his sleeve for a moment, then pulled out a scrap of paper. "I was hoping to find a clue to who wrote it. Had my suspicions, anyway, after it turned out to be a dead trail."

"So have I." Shadow took the note. It said simply, "News of Shadow can be had at Elaria's Herbal."

Shadow pulled out the list Elaria had given her and compared the papers. The paper looked identical, as did the handwriting.

"It *was* a trick, then," Aubry growled, looking over her shoulder. "Where'd you get that other piece?"

"From Elaria," Shadow said absently. "Somebody set you up to get their information for them."

"Do you know who it was?" Aubry asked cautiously.

"I've got a pretty good idea," Shadow said flatly, looking into Aubry's eyes. "Do you?"

"Uh—Shadow—" Aubry began uncomfortably.

"That's what I thought. Never mind." Shadow shrugged. "Probably better if you don't get involved, anyway. But I'll keep the note, if you don't mind."

"Go ahead." Aubry flushed and looked at his feet. "Listen, Shadow, if I thought I'd do any good—"

"Don't bother about it." Shadow tucked the two notes away in her sleeve. "You'd better leave first, and I'll go another way. I doubt anybody's seen us together."

"But how will I find you?" Aubry asked unhappily.

"I guess you won't, will you?" Shadow shrugged again. "Safer that way. Nobody'll think you're taking sides. Go on now."

"Shadow—" Aubry began, but she had already turned and was trotting down another alleyway.

She headed for Guild Row by way of the market, knowing that she would need money and probably plenty of it. There was no time for artistry, and she found her quick work unsporting, but by the time she reached Guild Row her sleeves were satisfyingly heavy and, more importantly, the work had helped her take her mind off her irrational disappointment at Aubry's perfectly logical desire to stay safely neutral. Shadow removed the bracelet and tucked it away inside her shirt, and began looking for the Black Lotus.

The tavern was neither hidden nor obvious, but it was certainly cleaner than the run of taverns in the area. It was half-full, and its clientele immediately put Shadow on alert. They were neither rich-looking and rowdy like the nobles at the Gildensword, nor scruffy and good-natured like the crowd at the Three-Spangled Horn. The patrons of the Black Lotus were dressed neatly and unobtrusively, and most sat alone. They drank quietly, watching Shadow with serpentine eyes.

Shadow took a deep breath and walked to the bar; there was no one else sitting there. The barkeep, a swarthy human male, padded silently over to meet her.

"What'll you have?" he asked tonelessly.

"Dragon's Blood," Shadow said quietly.

His expression never changed.

"There's Dragon's Blood and Dragon's Blood," he shrugged. "What year?"

"I'll have the vintage that Tigan drinks," she said. She pulled a pouch out of her sleeve and laid it on the counter.

The barkeep looked at her probingly, raising one eyebrow.

"That particular vintage don't come cheap," he warned.

"I've got expensive taste." Shadow shrugged. "I can pay."

The man scooped up the pouch and hefted it.

"Aye," he said at last. "I'll have to get it from down cellar. Come along, and see you're not cheated."

"All right."

Shadow followed the barkeep down a short hallway, then down a curving flight of stairs. He opened a door, showing Shadow a tiny room with only a table and four chairs. There was a lamp on the table, which the man lit. It gave off only the dimmest light.

"Wait here," he said.

Shadow nodded and sat down. The barkeep closed the door behind her, and Shadow heard the lock click. She reached for the lamp, but found that it could not be adjusted to give more light. Nervously, she drew one of her daggers and began tossing it from hand to hand.

"The least he could've done," Shadow muttered to herself, "was left some wine."

Time passed and Shadow grew more nervous. She had nothing to go on but Uncle's word. Still, what had she to lose? The locked door was nothing, even without the bracelet, and what difference between an assassin on her trail and one or more possibly outside the door?

At last she heard footsteps in the hall outside. A key grated in the lock and the barkeep entered, followed by a tall figure hidden in a gray robe and cowl. The barkeep laid a tray of wine and cheese on the table, then left. The gray-robed figure sat down opposite Shadow.

"Are you Tigan?" Shadow asked awkwardly.

"Perhaps." The voice was low and muffled.

"You'll pardon me," Shadow said ruefully. "I haven't done much of this type of dealing. But as I want to deal with Tigan, I'd rather not be more plain until I know—"

"If there is no bargain," the voice said reasonably, "then it hardly matters who I am. Who told you to ask for Tigan?"

"A beggar named Uncle, near the marketplace."

"Describe him."

"Human, old. Rag over the left eye." Shadow shrugged. "Missing his right leg midway up from the knee. Has a crowd of urchins spotting for him."

There was a long moment of silence.

"I know you by rumor," the voice said. "I think the job you would ask of Tigan is one he would refuse."

Shadow sighed exasperatedly and reached for the wine.

"Games and more games," she said exasperatedly. "If I wanted to dance I'd go back to the Horn. I'm not going to ask anyone to off Blade. I'm not fool enough to throw my money away needlessly."

"Then we can bargain." The figure reached up a hand to pull off the gray cowl. "I'm Tigan."

Shadow looked at him curiously. The man was short for a human, tall for an elf. His ears were elvishly pointed, but he had what very few elves did—a beard. A mix, then, like Donya.

"I'm Shadow," she said. "Of course, you knew that. It might simplify things a bit if you'd tell me just what you do know."

Tigan's eyes, exactly matching his gray robe, gazed deeply into her own.

"Better yet," he said, "tell me what *you* know. My knowledge comes at a price."

"I have something that Ganrom—among others— wants." Shadow shrugged. "In fact, he wants it rather badly. Badly enough that I believe there's a —shall we say, agreement?—between Ganrom and Blade concerning me. I'd like to see that agreement terminated."

"Yet you are not hiring direct action," Tigan mused. "You are aware that Blade is unaffiliated, and that our High Council cannot command her actions?"

"I'd heard that," Shadow agreed. "It's too bad. What I want is to see this agreement revoked by the issuing party."

"Ah." Tigan broke off a piece of cheese. "A complicated issue."

"Rather simple, actually." Shadow grinned. "I want you to deliver a message to Ganrom for me. Tell him I've had the bracelet placed in safekeeping. If something happens to me, he'll never get it back; I've seen to that. Oh, I could be 'persuaded' to tell where it is, I know that, but by the time that happened, the bracelet would be delivered straight into Lord Sharl's hands. If, on the other hand, he'd like to revoke the contract on me, I'll have the bracelet delivered to him in seven days."

"Why seven days?" Tigan asked curiously.

"It gives me time to see that Ganrom's keeping his side of the bargain, or to take steps if he doesn't." Shadow shrugged. "I'm aware that Blade can follow me just about anywhere I go, but once Ganrom has the bracelet and I leave town, there's no reason he should press the issue."

"How will you know he has complied?"

"Because I want Blade to deliver the contract herself," Shadow told him. "She can choose the place. As I said, if Ganrom cheats me and kills me, he'll never get the bracelet. It's to his advantage to do as I say."

"You're aware that he will keep a watch on you, to be sure you don't leave town," Tigan warned.

"I know. But I won't be leaving town until delivery, not as long as the contract's canceled."

"Don't you find a bracelet thin ransom for your life?" Tigan chuckled mirthlessly.

"Rather." Shadow shrugged. "But I've only got two choices, and I like that one better than the other. Otherwise, I believe a contract's canceled if the issuer turns up dead. If Ganrom won't bargain, then I've got to consider other arrangements."

"I see." Tigan swirled the wine in his cup. "I find myself wondering why you need me at this point. Any messenger could do what you ask."

"Any messenger could be bought off to tell whatever I'd told him," Shadow said. "Besides, if you're as good as I hear, Ganrom will also know how good you are. I trust you to deliver my message in such a way that Ganrom knows I've considered *both* ways to have the contract revoked . . . and that I haven't entirely discarded my other choice."

Tigan barely smiled.

"You are canny, my lady thief," he said. "I find your reasoning good. Shall we talk terms?"

"One thousand," Shadow offered.

"Twelve."

"I don't want you to *kill* him." Shadow laughed. "Not if he'll bargain. Two thousand."

"It would be easier to kill him. Ten thousand."

"It might be easier, but I doubt it'd be cheaper," Shadow retorted. "Four thousand."

"Eight thousand, half in advance."

"Five thousand, half in advance, and another thousand if Ganrom goes for it," Shadow said firmly.

Tigan considered.

"Done," he said at last. "I'll have the contract drawn up as soon as you can pay the advance."

Shadow patted her sleeve. The gems she had stolen since entering Allanmere jingled quietly.

"Got pen and paper?" She grinned.

Tigan raised an eyebrow.

"You're carrying that much money on you?" he asked. "You enjoy taking risks, don't you?"

"Yes," Shadow said simply. "But I also like working with professionals. Your advance is in unset gems, untraceable. You can have them appraised elsewhere before the job, if you want."

"No need," Tigan said easily. "We both know it would be unwise for you to cheat me. As you say, it's easy working with professionals." He drew pen, ink and parchment from a drawer under the table and wrote.

Shadow read the contract, nodded and signed, handing over the gems and the paper. Tigan pocketed the scroll and the pouch.

"Now, unless there's anything more?" he said.

"Any idea when the job might be done?" Shadow asked.

"I don't want to pressure you, but there's a certain amount of rush involved from my angle."

"Check here tomorrow. Mazak—he's the barkeep—he'll have word. You'll know anyway, though. How's Blade going to find you to deliver the contract?"

"Oh, please." Shadow laughed. "Blade? She's been following me for days."

Tigan also laughed.

"You're probably right. As I said, check tomorrow."

Shadow grinned.

"You're a quick worker."

"About some things, maybe," Tigan corrected.

SIX ═══════

From the Black Lotus, Shadow headed directly for the castle at a brisk trot. She veered east, however, out the North Gate, and found the hidden door Donya had shown her. It was locked, but Shadow had her tools and left the bracelet concealed in her shirt. From the door, it was a more difficult passage to Donya's room, but Shadow remembered the way and found it embarrassingly easy to avoid the servants and guards. The rooms were empty; Shadow kicked off her boots, lay down on the bed, and promptly fell asleep.

"*Damn* it, Shady!"

Shadow blinked, grinning sheepishly as she resheathed the dagger which had leaped reflexively to hand. Donya was standing by the edge of the bed, relief and anger warring in her expression.

"How did you get in here? And where have you been?" Donya demanded. "I've been all over the city, even to that pesthole of a Guildhouse! I've been to more inns and taverns than the busiest whore in town—"

"Calm down," Shadow laughed. "Scold me later."

"Well, Fortune spit on you, I've been worried!" Donya scowled. "I didn't know whether you'd been killed in some lice pit or just left town or—have you been all right?"

"Uncomfortable, but fine. I thought it might be a good idea to let things cool down a little. According to Argent, though, they haven't."

"I'll say not." Donya sat down on the edge of the bed. "Shady, just how much trouble *are* you in?"

"Ah, I'll manage." Shadow grinned and reached for the bottle of wine on the nightstand. "Needs refilling."

"I'll ring for some." Donya reached for the bell cord, but Shadow stopped her.

"Better not," she said regretfully. "I don't want anyone to know I'm here. That's why the sneaky entrance."

"Then you shouldn't have been napping on my bed. So wait in the dressing room. Have you eaten?"

"Not much."

Donya rang for wine and food, and when they had been brought, watched Shadow eat.

"You eat like you've been doing trail rations for a week," Donya said worriedly.

"Just about that," Shadow admitted. "Listen, are you still willing to do me a couple of favors?"

"You know I am."

Shadow pulled the bracelet out of her shirt and handed it over.

"Can you stash that for a while?" she asked. "Somewhere *really* safe. If it turns up, I'm worm food."

Donya looked at her soberly, then nodded.

"All right," she said. "I swear it'll be safe. What else?"

"You'll be getting a duplicate of that bracelet in a few days," Shadow told her. "I'll need it as soon as it gets here. I'm staying with Argent at his house. Also, I want to leave a thousand Suns with you. Just in case—well, anything happens, have the thousand Suns sent to Aspen in the Heartwood by way of any elf heading that way. Then you and your family can decide what had better be done with the bracelet."

"Aspen! So that's where you've been," Donya said exasperatedly. "All right, I'll do it. But I don't like this 'just in case' business. And I *still* don't know what's going on, and I don't like that, either. Not with the city boiling like water in a dragon's gullet."

Shadow sighed.

"You're better out of it, Doe, bet on it. It's a tangled mess, all right, and I'm only starting to unravel a few stray ends."

"This all has something to do with you, doesn't it?" Donya demanded. "This business with the temples and the Guild. It all goes back to the bracelet somehow, doesn't it?"

Shadow sighed again and looked into Donya's troubled eyes.

"Believe me, Doe, if I knew anything concrete I'd tell you. Right now I don't have any answers, just a lot of questions. And right at the moment I'm more concerned with my own skin than the city, if you'll pardon me."

"Well, if you can't tell me, you can't." Donya frowned. "But tell me this—it's bigger than you thought at first, isn't it?"

"And getting bigger all the time," Shadow agreed ruefully. "I don't know whether I somehow started the pot boiling or just fell into the soup by accident."

"Shadow . . . " Donya hesitated. "You know I'd never do anything to hurt you, but if it came down to open hostilities between the Guild and the Council of Churches . . . "

"I know." Shadow nodded. "As daughter of the High Lord and Lady, it'd be your duty to stand against the party who started it, and that looks like Ganrom and the Guild, doesn't it? And me, of course."

Donya nodded soberly. "You do understand." She sighed. "But as I said—"

"I know," Shadow said affectionately. "Don't worry, Doe. Before I'd let events put us on opposite sides I'd quit the Guild or leave town, you know that."

"I know," Donya said with relief. "But I'm glad to hear you say so. Isn't there anything I can do to help?"

"Maybe. It's a risk, but would your mother still be willing to do a little work for me?"

"I'm sure she will, if she can. And it's not too illegal," Donya added quickly. "Shall I ask her to meet us in her workroom? I think we can get you there without anyone seeing you."

"Great." Shadow nodded. "And it's nothing illegal, I promise. All open and aboveboard."

"If it is, it'll be the first time," Donya said grimly.

"This is starleaf tincture," Celene said, taking a last sniff from the tiny bottle. "I've only come across it once before. It's fantastically rare. You've a treasure here, kinswoman, and one I wouldn't mind making you an offer for myself."

"I can't very well sell it." Shadow laughed. "For once it's an honest gift. But what *is* starleaf tincture?"

"Why, a healing draught of great potency," Celene said, blinking. "A tiny sip will heal almost any wound, and counteract any poison. A few of the more remote elvan tribes used to make it, but starleaf was never very common, and these days I doubt if anyone could find any. It was far over-harvested during the wars."

"Hmmm. The person who gave it to me could find it, or grow it, if there was any to be found," Shadow mused, tucking the bottle back into its pouch, which she hung around her neck. "Handy thing to have!"

"Indeed it is. But what do you want done with these?" Celene asked, touching the two scraps of paper.

"You know, I'm not really sure," Shadow said, tossing a dagger thoughtfully. "I know there isn't enough there for a true divination, but these two notes are the only clue I've got to someone who's been following me for quite awhile, and I haven't even managed a look at whoever it is. Can you get anything out of them that'll give me any help at all?"

Celene frowned doubtfully, then her face cleared.

"I can give you a sort of warning device," she said. "It is the very simplest of spells, but it might do. The notes will be destroyed, though."

"That doesn't matter." Shadow shrugged. "They won't do me any good otherwise."

Celene rummaged through her shelves until she found a shallow silver dish, and placed the notes in it.

"I will need three strands of your hair, and three drops of your blood," she said, shuffling through her herb jars. "Just put them in the dish."

Shadow grimaced but unpinned one braid and plucked three hairs from it. She spit on her dagger tip and wiped it fastidiously on her tunic edge before pricking her finger and squeezing three ruby drops into the dish.

"That's fine."

Celene took a candle from the wall sconce. She began chanting and threw a pinch of something into the dish; the fire flared briefly, then turned green. Celene ended her chant and let the fire burn down on its own. She scraped the ashes carefully into a tiny glass vial, which she stoppered and handed to Shadow.

"This will glow brightly in the presence of the one who wrote the notes," she said. "It will also become quite hot, and the glow and the heat will increase with proximity. It hasn't much range, only about fifty paces."

"Detectable?" Shadow asked.

"I should think not; such very elementary magic usually goes overlooked," Celene said thoughtfully. "Most detection spells focus on specific types of magic—protection or defense spells, actual divination, illusion, and so on. This is a rather elementary bit of sympathetic magic."

She gave Shadow a stern look.

"I would much prefer to know," she said, "precisely why you want this spell and how you plan to use it. Donya assures me that it is nothing wrongful and I'll trust you for that, but I would rather know, for my own peace of mind."

"Simple enough." Shadow shrugged. "Somebody's been following me around, as I said. While I was visiting some kinfolk in the forest, someone—the same person or someone else—was asking about me in a rather sneaky way, and wrote these notes. I want to find out who's following me and why, who's asking about me and why, and whether they're the same person. Anybody going to that much trouble probably isn't looking for me to just say hello and pass the time of day, you know."

"I hope no one intends you harm?" Celene asked anxiously.

"I hope not myself," Shadow said innocently, chuckling to herself as she reviewed the list of those in Allanmere who probably did.

"Perhaps you didn't exaggerate the risks you faced in the Guild believing you an informer," Celene said, frowning. "I'd not like to think that your visits here have placed you in danger."

"If that's it, I'll find out," Shadow said vaguely.

"I see you're no longer wearing that bracelet," Celene observed.

"It was becoming too much of a—bone of contention," Shadow told her. "So I put it in safekeeping."

"I hope it *is* truly safe," Celene said worriedly.

"There's no safer place," Shadow said firmly, earning a warm smile from her friend.

"Perhaps you could appeal to Guildmaster Ganrom," Celene suggested. "He's made a great deal of trouble in council these days, but as your Guildmaster, perhaps he might be best able to help you."

"Maybe," Shadow agreed neutrally. "I've sent him a message about it already."

Donya looked at her sharply, and Shadow realized that while she might be able to double-talk Celene, Donya already knew that neither the problem nor its solution would be that simple. She'd best be careful—she couldn't keep hedging her friend forever, and Donya had better never learn that Shadow was trafficking with assassins! Questions of loyalty and law aside, Donya would most likely rush out to take Blade on herself, and humans' lives were so pathetically short anyway.

"And there is always the City Guard," Celene offered. "True, it would be odd for a Guild member to be dealing with the guard, but even so, you're entitled to the protection of law."

Shadow stifled a smile at the thought of a thief appealing to the City Guard for protection. Celene little knew how truly ineffectual the guard was, and as a loyal Guild member, it was hardly her place to bring it to the High Lady's attention!

"I appreciate your help," Shadow told her. "But if you'll forgive me, I'd best leave before someone gets suspicious."

Donya walked her back to the garden exit, making sure they were unobserved.

"You're sure there's nothing else I can do?" she asked at

last. Her eyes were dark with worry. "I liked it better when we fought together, back to back. I don't like feeling so useless."

"You're not useless, and I'm not helpless," Shadow said firmly. "I'm a tough, sly old thing. Remember Everfar?"

"I'll never forget it." Suddenly Donya pulled the signet ring off her little finger and held it out. "At least take this."

"Your signet? Come on, Doe—" Shadow protested.

Donya grabbed Shadow's hand and shoved the ring onto her middle finger, where it fit a little loosely.

"It's return-spelled," she said. "Most royal insignia are, just in case they're captured in battle. If either you or I say my name backwards, it'll return to me. Promise me you'll send it if you need help, Shady."

Shadow clenched her hand around the ring and swallowed hard against the sudden lump in her throat. Abruptly she hugged her friend fiercely.

"I promise," she said, her voice hoarse. "What did I ever do to deserve a friend like you?"

"I guess you tempted Fortune's left hand once too often," Donya returned, her voice just as hoarse. "You take care now."

"And you." Shadow turned and hurried through the gate as quickly as she could, afraid she might embarrass herself if she looked back.

Fortunately the castle sided on the northeast edge of the Noble District. Unfortunately, the Noble District, unlike other parts of the town, had been purposely built to avoid the chancy, dark alleys which Shadow preferred for discreet travel. It was difficult to pass unnoticed, and there were no shops to duck into quickly. Shadow worriedly contemplated the walk to Argent's; until Tigan managed to get to Ganrom, tonight at the earliest, the contract on her permitted Blade to act at any moment.

She pulled out the glass vial and consulted it. The ashes were glowing faintly, and the glass was slightly warmer than could be accounted for by the warmth of Shadow's hand. Fifty paces?

"Dragon droppings," Shadow swore softly. As casually as she could, she lounged against the side of a building and took a quick look around. The market crowds were returning home, and nobles were starting to make their way to taverns and clubs. There were any number of people about, including many tall, dark human women. Shadow quickly tucked the vial into her breastband where she could not fail to feel any change in temperature, thus freeing both hands.

"Fortune favor me," Shadow murmured, a little more prayerfully than usual. She stepped boldly out into the street, walking quickly and purposefully, staying in plain view. The vial grew no hotter, but neither did it cool.

She worried as she walked. She couldn't afford to lead Blade to Argent's house; neither could she afford to stall about the street, giving the assassin any number of opportunities. In attempting to lose her follower, she would have to also lose her open and visible position, which was probably the only thing keeping Blade from attacking.

There was the potion Chyrie had given her. If Blade's attack wasn't immediately fatal and she could get to the vial, perhaps she could let Blade think she was dead.

A moment's thought, however, dashed that hope. Blade was a professional assassin, and one of her reputation would certainly make *sure* of her success. Supposed victims turning up alive and well could be quite embarrassing! In any event, Shadow could ill afford to take the risk that Blade's attack would leave her alive long enough to use the potion.

The vial grew slightly warmer. There was a large crowd of noble youths ahead, standing about and offering com-

ments and jeers to a vegetable merchant and his three slaves
attempting to change a broken wagon wheel. Ordinarily, it
would have been an ideal opportunity for a little quick
money—everyone in the area had their attention on the
scene—but Shadow had little interest at the moment. Unless
she could lose Blade in that crowd, perhaps—

Abruptly the vial flared white-hot, drawing a yelp of pain
from Shadow. She slapped at the vial, distracted, and
caught a roughness in the road, stumbling and falling to her
knees.

A black blur flashed scant inches above her head, and
Shadow wasted no time on reflection. She threw herself
down and sideways, rolling head over heels and coming up
on her feet. A tall figure in black was moving toward her.
The face was a blur—Shadow caught a brief impression of
short dark hair framing a pale face—but the shining black
dagger in one hand was crystal clear.

Shadow dove without thought for the crowd around the
wagon. She slithered through silk and velvet-clad legs,
provoking curses, yelps and protests as she went, feeling
the vial still hot as her pursuer followed close behind.

There was the wagon, two slaves holding up one corner
while the third maneuvered the wheel into place. Without
hesitation, Shadow scuttled under the wagon, muttering a
quick apology as she elbowed both slaves sharply in the
groin. Two shouts of pain, and the unsupported corner of
the wagon came crashing down, peppers and onions cas-
cading out of it. The bottom of the wagon whacked Shadow
sharply on the head, and bright lights flashed across her
vision, but she could not hesitate. Immediately she was up
on the far side of the wagon.

Out of the corner of her eye she saw a black-clad figure
struggling with nobles, the wagon and fallen vegetables, but
Shadow dared not wait. She dashed down the street,

rounded a corner and then another without taking note of directions, and used a lean-to shed to make for the roofs. Almost recklessly she leaped from one rooftop to the next until she recognized Argent's house. She paused, ducking behind one of the chimneys, until she ascertained that the vial was completely cold, then immediately climbed into the sooty opening.

Smoke rose to choke her, and the brick was almost hot enough to burn. Shadow braced back and feet against the walls and began working her way down as quickly as she could without falling. The heat increased, and the seat of her pants became quite uncomfortably hot. Her eyes were streaming so that it was difficult to place her feet, and it was impossible to see how much further she had to go.

POP! A log exploded somewhere beneath her, and suddenly the seat of her pants was no longer just hot—it was blazing. Shadow jerked sharply and her feet came loose. Her back scraped painfully on the chimney blocks as she fell, only to land with a crash directly on the fire!

"YEEEOOOW!"

Shadow sprang up from her uncomfortable seat and crashed directly into Argent, who was hurrying over, sending them both tumbling to the floor.

"Shadow? What—" Argent began dazedly.

"MY PANTS!" Shadow yowled, rolling over the rug.

Argent immediately slapped at the flames, a process which, however successful, added nothing to Shadow's comfort. As soon as the blaze was out, Shadow pulled away and hurried for the front door, fishing in her tunic front as she did so.

The vial was cool, or at least as cool as could be expected under the circumstances, and remained so at all sides of the house. Only after Shadow had tested each entrance and looked carefully out the windows did she finally sigh with relief and slouch, panting, against the wall.

"Shadow, what in the Mother Forest is the matter with you?" Argent said exasperatedly. "Has it *ever* occurred to you to come to the front door of a building and knock? Just look at yourself!"

Shadow walked over to a polished shield mirror (leaving a black smudge on the white wall where she'd leaned), and had to laugh. The entire back and most of one leg of her pants were burned away, and her tunic was torn in several places. She was covered with soot from top to toe, and where there was no soot she was smeared with mud and manure from the road. Her hair was half-undone and hanging down in dirty black ropes around her face, framing a bloody lump on the top of her head.

Almost immediately her laughter turned to coughs, and Argent's expression of annoyance gave way to concern.

"Never mind for now," he said quickly. "Let's get you into a bath and I'll see to your head."

The hot water of Argent's bathing pool was painful on Shadow's scorched flanks, but she scrubbed ruthlessly at hair and hide until the last traces of dirt and soot were gone. Argent brought a cold compress for her head and soothing lotion for her burns, and at last, wrapped (or rather, buried) in one of Argent's robes and armed with a mug of cold ale, Shadow was able to relax and tell Argent about the attempt on her life.

Argent only shook his head ruefully when she had finished.

"And I thought you were exaggerating your danger this morn," he said with a sigh. "Nonetheless, after you left I remembered that you had no key to my home, so I left Elaria to run the shop and came directly back. I've given the

servants a holiday, so the house should be secure enough,
but what will you do now?"

"Nothing tonight." Shadow sighed. "I don't even have
any clothes. Tomorrow I've got to check back with somebody for news. I'm hoping that by then there won't be
anything to worry about."

Argent looked at her probingly.

"Should I ask?"

"No, better not." Shadow smiled wanly. "If I'd been
thinking straight, I probably wouldn't have accepted your
offer to stay here, but it came at the right time, unfortunately for you."

Argent sat silent for a long moment, then shook his head
again.

"You're probably hungry," he said. "I hope you don't
mind cold food, as I sent the cook home with the rest.
Unless you can cook?"

"Me?" Shadow chuckled. "I can prop something over a
fire if I'm starving. Anything more complicated than that
and we *will* starve. But I don't suppose you have anything
I could wear? This robe of yours would make me three
outfits."

"I might have something old of Elaria's," Argent said
doubtfully.

"Elaria must have five handspans on me," Shadow
laughed. "Anything of hers is going to fit me like warhorse
barding on a pony. Never mind, I'll figure something out
tomorrow. Come on, let's see what's in the pantry—and,
more importantly, the wine cellar."

This mission was somewhat comically accomplished, for
Argent's robe was almost two feet too long in the hem and
the sleeves, and after nearly breaking her neck on the stairs,
Shadow tossed it aside and continued in her bare skin (not
entirely to Argent's displeasure). After a feast of bread,

cheese, cold mutton and wine, Shadow opted for another
bath.

"I could fall in love with your bathing pool." She sighed,
luxuriating in the bubbly water. "In all my travels, I've only
found three cities with hot springs piped in. After spending
most of the last week on the road—sometimes literally—I
can't imagine anything better. Well, almost nothing."

She opened one eye to give Argent a significant look.

"I can't understand why you haven't picked a city and
settled down," Argent suggested. "You seem fond of your
comfort."

"Ah, I have itchy feet," Shadow said with a shrug.
"Besides, I make friends too easily."

"Thus hurting your profits?" Argent guessed.

"Oh, that, too," Shadow said. "But I *like* humans, Argent.
Sometimes too well. They're endlessly entertaining—well,
I'm sure you know that, working in Allanmere. It's hard to
stay around and watch them grow old and feeble and finally
die. When Donya and I parted company two years ago in
Mountaindale, frankly I never expected to see her again. It's
easier that way, I think."

"But to lose every human you befriend—" Argent
protested.

"Oh, I don't *lose* them," Shadow said uncomfortably. "I
remember them, you know." She grinned. "Anyway, I
make friends easily, as I said."

She climbed out of the tub and toweled off briskly, taking
Argent's hand to lead him back to the bedroom, where she
picked up a bottle of wine and lounged on the hearth rug.

"With your occupation, and what looks like a propensity
for getting into trouble, I don't see how you've managed to
outlive anybody," Argent said amusedly. "At the present, I
imagine Donya rather worries the same about you."

"Oh, Donya's a worrier." Shadow chuckled. "But I'm

stubborn, you know. Nobody sends *me* back to the Mother Forest before I'm good and ready to go!"

"I believe that." Argent sat down on the hearth rug next to Shadow and began unbraiding her hair. "All the same, how can you be sure I'm not among those conspiring against you?"

"You?" Shadow laughed. "Sorry, Argent, no offense, but I wouldn't bet a tarnished copper on your success in anything sneaky. You're altogether too gentle and trusting. Besides, you're sunk in too deep at the castle, and Donya's a much better judge of character than I am."

"I should probably take that as an insult, but I'll let it pass," Argent said mildly. "And I must agree with you regarding Donya's judgment, if you represent her choice in friends. Do you know, you never did tell me the story she mentioned—Everfar, wasn't it?"

"Oh, Fortune favor me." Shadow groaned. "I thought you'd have forgotten about that."

"Come now," Argent said coaxingly. "Don't you owe me that story, at least?"

"I suppose I do." Shadow sighed. "All right, then. But you've got to promise me you won't tell anybody. It's embarrassing enough now."

"I swear by leaf and vine." Argent grinned. "Go on."

"Well, this was a ways back, when Donya was traveling about a bit," Shadow said, remembering. "We hadn't met too many months before. I thought she was mostly something of an idiot. I could tell she was born to money. Oh, she never said anything about being a High Lord's daughter, you can be sure of that—but anybody who'd been on the road as long as I could smell the highborn twenty yards away. I couldn't imagine why anybody who had a choice would be making their way as a hire-sword. Of course I didn't ask; Fortune knew it wasn't any of my business, anyway. As I said, though, we'd become good enough friends, and it was plain to me that Donya was out there to prove something to herself, so I thought I'd stick around a while, just to see she didn't get into any trouble, you know. So, as things go, we'd made our way for a few months, as I said, hiring on here and there in various capacities; she as a guard or some such, and I as whatever I could manage. I'm good at any number of things," Shadow added modestly.

"So I've seen." Argent laughed affectionately.

"Anyway, on this particular occasion we'd hired on with a merchant caravan passing through a large forest. Donya thought the caravan was a little bare of guards for the cargo it was taking, but the merchants were rather stingy, I suppose. So there we were with Donya and only half-dozen other guards, and maybe twenty others in a caravan of eight wagons.

"We got along fair enough the first few days, but on the fifth day out I smelled something nasty on the wind. Fortune knows what was bothering me, but I was as edgy as a she-fox in heat, and Donya'd caught a little of it from me. She was sticking pretty close, as I was riding in the lead wagon, and we both had our eyes out sharp, but still it took us cold when at least fifteen bandits came whooping out of the forest, bows spitting and swords a-swinging.

"As I said, I'd been half-expecting trouble, and I just tumbled back into the wagon where the arrows couldn't get at me, peeped out through a crack, and let Donya do what she does best—that is, swing her own sword. The damned thing's bigger than I am. So she was swinging away like a good one, and I saw at least two of the bandits go down before a couple of them hopped into the wagon and found me. I'm a dirty fighter—when you're as small as me, mostly you choose between coming out honorably and coming out alive—but they were big and strong and rather nasty fighters themselves, and before long one of them fetched me a good rap on the head, and out I went.

"When I came around I was tied tight as a Festival goose to a tree, and most of the bandits were swilling some of the merchants' wine around a fire while some of them went through the chests. I could see that there were a few of them dead on the ground nearby, but mostly they were all there. Donya may have made a good fight of it, but they'd got her in the end, and she was tied up tight as me, but in a more uncomfortable position—they'd tied her hands to her feet behind her—a few trees over. She was bruised and banged up worse than me, but she wasn't badly hurt, and she was watching me through slitted eyes. She nodded at the bandits, then closed her eyes again, and I guessed what she meant, that they didn't know we were awake yet. So I closed my eyes to slits and listened, and learned. The others were dead; I'd figured as much when I didn't see them. They'd kept Donya and me for purposes I'm sure you can guess; they figured on a jolly tumble among the lot of them, first Donya, then me. Also, they hadn't managed to find the lead wagon's main cache and were disappointed in the haul.

"Time went by and the bandits started getting impatient waiting for us to wake up, so one of them came over and started slapping me around a bit. I thought it politic to open my eyes and 'wake up.' Donya received the same treatment. They gave us some water and food—one of the bandits feeding us—and then left us for a bit while they ransacked the chests again.

"I looked over and saw that, uncomfortable and battered as she was, Donya was making the best of the situation. She was working her bonds against her spurs, carefully, when nobody was looking. But trying to hide her movements, tied as she was, it was slow going. The bandits would be over for a tumble with her first, long before she'd make it. That meant there was nothing to be done but buy some time.

"Well, I've never been the shy sort. I sat up straight and called over, 'You know, it's bad enough to interrupt a fellow thief at her work, and knock her about the head and truss her to a tree, but to sit there when there's wine about and give me water, well, that's the sorriest thing I've ever heard, especially when I could do you quite a good turn.'

" 'Oh, you'll do us a good enough turn, by and by,' one of the bandits said, and laughed.

" 'I don't mind,' I said, 'But I can do you a better one still, if you'll let me up a bit.'

" 'And what good turn's that, hey?' he said. 'Tell, and maybe we'll untie you for a bit.'

" 'I can show you where the merchant hid his sack,' I told him. 'I would've had it myself in a day or two, and been off, but that you interrupted me at what I thought was one of the prettiest setups I've ever done. But things as they are, I'll tell you where it is, and not ask even so much as a share, if you'll just let me go with a whole hide.'

" 'And what of her, eh?' the bandit challenged, nodding at Donya, who'd gone stone-still.

" 'You can do what you want with her.' I shrugged. 'What do I care for a human bitch? I was along for a chance at the cash, I tell you. And you can all have at her night and day, for all of me, but you won't touch me after; she's tumbled every man in the train, and gave them all whore's-rot.'

"Well, that made them listen," Shadow continued, "and one of them cut me loose, watching sharp while I found the right chest. And there was the sack just where I knew it was, in a false lid—"

"But how did you know where it was?" Argent asked.

"Oh, well," Shadow said embarrassedly, "I *am* a thief,

after all, and, well, it's something of a habit to keep an eye out."

"Surely you weren't planning to rob your employer?" Argent asked, shocked.

"Oh, I wasn't *planning* anything of the sort." Shadow laughed. "But as to whether or not I'd have done it if an opportunity came up—well, I wouldn't like to be asked that question under truthspell."

"So then what happened?"

"Well, the leader was rather impressed by that, especially as I had to bypass a rather nasty poison needle, spring mounted, to get at the sack," Shadow said modestly. "That convinced them, at least, that I *was* a thief, and they were a tad more friendly after that. So they passed the wine and the food around, and I found some dreamweed among the stores, but when I managed to get a look at Donya I could see it was slow going with the rope; and then, of course, how was I going to get away even when she was free? So I tried to keep the bandits busy telling jokes and stories, and drinking and smoking, but that wasn't going to hold them all night, and I wasn't sure they'd bought my story about Donya, either.

"So up I got and asked if any of them could play an instrument, and it turned out that one played the pipes—not very well, I'm here to say—and another was passable enough on some stringed thing that I didn't recognize. So they played, and I got up there and danced the High Circle—"

"The High Circle," Argent mused. "It's been a long time since I saw that one."

"You've been living in the city too long." Shadow laughed. "Truth is, elves in my clan always had a hard time getting pregnant, and we used to make quite a ceremony of it. When a few of us came ripe, we'd haul all the available fellows out to the forest altars and dance the High Circle, asking the Mother Forest to make us ripe and their seed strong. So it was a fertility dance, but I'd say the main purpose was to get the men interested. Anyway, it was working on those bandits, bet on it! And by the time I was done, not a one of them knew that Donya existed. And Donya managed to get loose without them noticing, and found some Purple Sleep and sneaked the juice into the wine—I didn't know about it—and come morning the lot of us were sleeping like hibernating bears, and Donya just dragged me away."

"But all those bandits," Argent protested. "A pack of filthy, brutal humans is hardly a High Circle dance!"

"Oh, humans take that kind of thing worse than elves do, you should know that." Shadow shrugged uncomfortably. "It wasn't so bad, except for all the lice I picked up. Besides, by that time I'd had so much wine and dreamweed that I wouldn't have noticed if it was a gargoyle in my pallet. And we got all the bandits' horses and as much of the caravan's cargo as we could carry away, and we sold all of it in the next town, so it wasn't a total loss, after all."

Argent shook his head slowly.

"I can see," he said, "why Donya places such value on your friendship. A good judge of character, indeed."

"Well, story for story," Shadow said firmly. "I've had a question on my mind for a few days now, and maybe you'll know something being so close with Donya's parents."

"What question is that?" Argent said warily. "That you couldn't ask Donya, that is."

"I thought elf-human matings always gave out twins, one mostly human and one mostly elvan," Shadow speculated. "Now, I *know* Donya wouldn't have been allowed to run all over the place playing hire-sword if she was the High Lord's only heir. But *now* she's Heir, and I can see she's not delighted by it. What happened to her twin?"

Argent frowned uncomfortably.

"I don't know, exactly," he said. "Danyel, as you might have guessed, was the more elvish of the two, and little like Donya—rather a scholarly sort, quiet. By Allanmere tradition, Danyel was fostered among some of the forest elves, expecting to be Heir, as he was a few minutes older than his sister. He was more or less betrothed to an elvan girl, too, and seemed content enough. Then when Donya returned—it must have been just after she left you—he decided he wanted a taste of adventure and wandering himself. Sharl and Celene didn't like the idea at all, but they thought he'd be safe enough with his sister, so long as he wasn't gone too long.

"Whatever happened," Argent said slowly, "it is not spoken of. Donya returned three months later without her brother. She was—well, changed. For months she never left the castle, staying secluded in heavy mourning. There's little doubt he's dead—the family held his funeral—but his body was not returned. Donya was declared Heir, and she's not left Allanmere since, and Danyel's name hasn't been spoken in court since she returned."

Shadow shook her head. "Yes, she's more serious than she used to be," she said. "I thought it was just being stuck in this city, doomed to rulership. Well, she'll tell me someday, or she won't. None of my affair, anyway. I've got enough things to worry about now."

"Indeed you have," Argent said firmly.

He spread the long ebony flow of Shadow's hair over her skin, where it shone in the firelight. Suddenly he seized her by the shoulders and flipped her over on the rug, then kissed her lingeringly.

"Argent!"

"Well, if you're going to wander around skin-bare, Shadow," Argent said, smiling, "and tell such stories as you told me, you must be prepared to take the consequences."

"Prepared?" Shadow laughed. "I'd been wondering what was taking you so long! Elves shouldn't own businesses, Argent. You've become much too self-controlled and polite."

"That sounds like a dare," Argent warned.

"Bet on it," Shadow said slyly. "Now come here and give me those consequences, eh?"

SEVEN

"I like it," Argent laughed.

Shadow was not so amused. One of Argent's shirts, the sleeves rolled up several times, fell past her knees. Its belted length somewhat concealed the fact that a pair of his trousers, hacked off nearly a foot above the cuff, came nearly up to her breasts, where it was tied securely. Twine also secured the bottom of the trouser legs, and she had wound the twine about her legs to keep the trousers from ballooning out comically.

She looked at her reflection and grimaced.

"It'll do," she said dismally, "until I can get to a clothes merchant. You know, sometimes I think Fortune's right hand may be on my head, but her left keeps a good grip on my clothes."

"Are you sure you should go out yet?" Argent asked gently. It was midafternoon. "You could stay out of sight here another day or so."

"Nah, I'm walking on nails till I get some news," Shadow said with a grin. "I'll be back tonight, unless I get my throat slit somewhere."

"I wish you wouldn't say things like that."

"Sorry." Shadow shrugged. "Don't worry about me, Argent. I'm due for some good luck."

"I could call a carriage for you."

"And parade me before every watchful eye in Allanmere in this getup?" Shadow laughed. "Any assassin on my trail might just laugh himself to death. No, thanks, I think I'd better be a little more discreet than that."

Shadow was discreet indeed, skirting the west edge of town until she found a clothes merchant and hurriedly exchanged Argent's hand-me-downs for more suitable clothing. Neither the vial nor her instincts told her that she was being followed, and she reached the Black Lotus without mishap.

Mazak eyed her without curiosity.

"What'll you have tonight?" he asked disinterestedly.

"Ale."

He pushed a mug and a paper over to her. Shadow opened the note. It said simply, "Negotiations were successful. Have remainder of fee delivered when desired document is received."

Shadow folded the paper and tore it into shreds; Mazak mutely swept the shreds into the waste barrel.

"Thanks." Shadow grinned. She pulled a pouch from her sleeve and placed it on the counter. "Fortune favor you, my friend."

Mazak raised one eyebrow but said nothing, merely stuffing the pouch into his pocket.

Shadow drained the mug in several huge swallows and let out an explosive sigh.

"Wonderful," she said. She beckoned Mazak closer; he leaned over the counter.

"Tell me something, friend," she said. "*Is* there really a liquor called Dragon's Blood?"

The other eyebrow shot up, and Mazak grinned broadly.

"Aye," he chuckled. "Strong as it sounds, and it ain't what you'd call precisely legal, nor what you'd call cheap, either."

"How much?" Shadow grinned. "I'm celebrating."

"Hundred Suns a glass, thousand a bottle."

"A hundred—" Shadow was stunned to silence, then she shrugged.

"Why not?"

She pulled out a pouch and counted out ten ten-Sun pieces, placing them on the counter.

Mazak chuckled again as he took the money, then disappeared into a back room. When he came out he held a small black bottle, from which he poured about a thimbleful of purple-black liquid into a tiny cup.

"A hundred Suns for that?" Shadow said incredulously. "Dragon's Blood, hah! I could have the whole carcass for twice that."

"Trust me, lady, you won't be wanting more at one go," Mazak nodded. "Go on, take it down."

Shadow contemplated the cup dubiously for a moment, then shrugged and raised it to her lips, tilting the liquid into her mouth.

Instantly her tongue and throat caught fire, the flame following the draught down to her stomach where a small explosion resulted. An equally delightful and potent aroma spread out over her taste buds. Shadow coughed violently, knuckling tears from her eyes, and clutched the edge of the bar as the fiery liquor shot straight to her head.

"Whoa!" she breathed. "Got any water?"

"Trust me, lady, you'll be wanting ale." Mazak laughed, pushing the mug to her. His laughter was faintly echoed by several of the watching patrons. "Water makes it worse."

Shadow took a tremendous gulp of ale, which partially

doused the fire in her throat and stomach but failed to make the world stand still. Waves of well-being and energy pulsed through her, and she sat still, holding onto the bar top, until the world settled a bit.

"Fortune favor me," Shadow said, wiping her eyes again, "That's the stuff!"

Mazak guffawed, and chuckles broke out around the room.

"So you like it, eh?"

"Like it?" Shadow shook her head ruefully. "Here's the thousand Suns; I'll take a bottle and embarrass myself in private. Not that I begrudge the entertainment, mind!"

"Perhaps you will spot a round for me."

The voice, coming from behind Shadow, was colorless but recognizably female. Mazak's eyes shot up, and all expression fled from his face. The room became abruptly silent.

Shadow's hands twitched, but she didn't turn around.

"Certainly," she said. "Shall we open the bottle here or somewhere else?"

"I have a room." The voice was faintly amused now. "I am unsure of my welcome here."

Shadow picked up the bottle of Dragon's Blood and turned, schooling her face to careful blankness.

The woman was as tall as Elaria had described her. Hair as black as Shadow's, but cut to shoulder length, framed a narrow, pale face and eyes so black that they made the hair look pale. Black also was her plain tunic, trousers and boots. She even wore black gloves and a black dagger at her hip, the only weapon Shadow could see.

Shadow rose and followed Blade out the door, conscious of hostile eyes upon them. They walked only a short way before entering a decrepit hostel and climbing some stairs to a room empty but for a table and two chairs.

Seemingly from nowhere, Blade produced two tiny crystal cups, and Shadow silently poured a small portion of Dragon's Blood into them. She sipped first, barely choking down her coughs; Blade, however, seemed unaffected as she swallowed her own drink.

"You have—" Shadow cleared her throat, "—something for me?"

The dark eyes were unreadable.

"Only my word," Blade said. "I have no written contract."

Shadow fought to keep her amazement out of her face. Professionals, whether assassins or thieves on hire, invariably required a contract. Some employers sought to dodge payment by reporting the hireling to the law after the job was done, or simply by threat of doing so. A written contract could be turned in to the City Guard, and the employer's signature, confirmed under spell, was damning evidence. Shadow knew that in Allanmere, at least, the penalty for assassination was death, but the penalty for *hiring* an assassin was death by torture.

"I have no need of contracts," Blade said blandly. "I enforce my own bargains. Fool is he who crosses me."

Looking at the dead black eyes, Shadow could well believe it. Something about that still face sent a needle of ice into her heart. She cleared her throat again.

"Then Ganrom revoked the con— the arrangement?" Shadow said quickly.

"He has." The barest flicker of annoyance crossed Blade's face, then was gone.

"If you had to refund the fee—" Shadow began, but Blade's humorless laugh interrupted her. The laugh made her shiver.

"Such fee as I charge," Blade said mildly, "is not subject to refund, nor did Ganrom presume to ask it. He is a fool, but a cautious fool. One day soon he will be a dead fool."

They were silent a moment, and Blade surveyed Shadow through narrowed eyes.

"The very gods bespoke your life yesterday," she said at last. "You are a nimble creature, and clever, but it is rare indeed that my dagger misses its mark."

She drew the black dagger from its sheath and toyed with it. It seemed to flicker in her hands like a thing alive, and Shadow shivered again.

"I'm sorry to disappoint you," Shadow said rather lamely. "But living has become something of a habit with me."

Blade did not smile. She flipped the dagger from hand to hand, just as Shadow habitually did.

"Indeed I was disappointed," she said, her eyes never leaving Shadow's. "I would have relished your life."

Abruptly she caught the dagger and sheathed it, on her feet in one smooth motion. Her walk was as lithe as a cat's, and she paused at the door.

"You owe me a life," Blade said, with the barest hint of a cold smile. "When you are ready to pay that debt, ask for black orchids at the vendor of flowers at the south end of the market." She closed the door behind her.

Shadow sat gaping in astonishment at the closed door for a moment. At last she poured herself a swallow of Dragon's Blood with hands that trembled; she tossed down the liquor, then coughed violently for a moment. By the time her eyes cleared, she was much calmer.

"Whoo!" she said at last, knuckling her eyes. "Lady Fortune, I may learn my lesson yet. For once, I do believe I'm *out of my depth*."

Despite what most would have considered a supernatural tolerance for liquor, after three doses of Dragon's Blood in less than an hour, Shadow was far from sober. She pocketed the bottle of Dragon's Blood—and the tiny cups—and stumbled back to the street.

Shadow chuckled to herself as she carefully set one foot in front of the other. It had been at least a decade since she'd been this drunk; and here on Guild Row, despite the cancellation of Blade's contract—agreement—she was far from safe!

Shadow found a post to lean against while she foggily considered her predicament. She wasn't quite sure she could make it back to Argent's unless she found a cart to take her there, and she'd scarcely find one on Guild Row. A sobering spell would be nice, but the only mage in the area, Aliendra, had made it plain that Shadow wasn't to set bootsole in her shop. If she could make it as far as the market—

"Shadow?" Aubry was there, his face drawn with concern. "Are you all right? What're you doing here?"

"Fine." Shadow belched. "I'm fine."

"Phew—no, you're not; you're drunk as a warrior back from a dragon hunt," Aubry grimaced. He pried Shadow's hand loose from the post and looped the arm over his shoulder, his other arm around Shadow's waist. She was so much shorter than he that this position lifted her to her toe-tips.

"Where're we going?" Shadow asked as they started down a street that seemed to lurch under her feet.

"My place," Aubry shrugged. "I can't think of anywhere else. You can't just stand around on Guild Row drunk. You'd just be begging for—ah, trouble."

"Like maybe a dagger between my shoulder blades?" Shadow guessed with a laugh. "Keep your secrets, Aubry, I've got other sources."

"Hush," Aubry said nervously. He dragged Shadow into a grubby inn, up a flight of creaking stairs, and into a small, untidy room. Shadow plopped limply onto the narrow bed and looked around disdainfully.

"Fortune's tits, Aubry." She grimaced. "Is this the best you can do? The damned Silver Dragon's only a Moon a day, and that was without bargaining."

Aubry scowled.

"It may not have occurred to you, Shadow," he said crossly, "but not all of us can strut into the market and come back with our sleeves dripping Suns every day, or cadge free feasts at the castle. Some of us poor beginners have to *work* to get by."

"Okay, okay." Shadow swung her legs over the edge of the bed, groaning at the effort, and scrubbed the heel of her hand across her eyes to clear them. She followed Aubry's glance to the signet on her finger.

"Mother Forest, is *that* what's eating at you?" she said at last. "You think I've got something going at the castle, eh?"

Aubry said nothing, but he could not meet her eyes.

"I'll bet fifty Suns Ganrom started that rumor, too, didn't he?" Shadow said triumphantly. "Well? Come on, I'll pay on the spot if I'm wrong."

Aubry's eyebrows raised.

"You know, I *did* hear it at the Guildhouse," he admitted. "But why—"

"To get someone else to do his Fortune-cursed dirty work for him, that's why," Shadow said, growling. "But here's the truth. Donya's an old friend of mine, and until I came here I didn't know a damned thing about her family. I've eaten their food and drank their wine, and damned near lifted the tableware, but I haven't taken so much as a copper from them, nor given them so much as a mouse's peep of information. Now you can tell that to anyone you please, and I'll defend it knife to knife in traditional style if you like."

Aubry was silent a long moment, looking into Shadow's eyes; then he sighed.

"I believe you," he said. "I'm sorry, Shady."

"Mother Forest," Shadow said, rolling her eyes. "Can't you do better than *that*?" She deliberately kicked off one boot, then the other.

"All right." Aubry laughed, moving to join Shadow on the bed. "I guess I can, at that."

" . . . but not until you put out that damned pipe!"

"All right, I'm a fat merchant," Shadow said patiently, knotting the pouch over her belt.

"Not very convincing." Aubry grinned.

Shadow shrugged and stuffed the pillow down the front of her tunic so that it bulged ludicrously.

"*Now* what are you going to do?" she asked, looking away deliberately.

"Laugh myself silly," Aubry said, but he obediently reached toward the pouch.

"Not that way, you cloud-headed twit," Shadow scolded. "You don't cut the pouch, you cut the thongs."

"But then he'll notice the difference in weight," Aubry protested.

"No more than he'd notice you tugging at his pouch for half the day. Now cut the thongs, and cut *up*, holding the bottom of the pouch, and then it won't pull."

Aubry sighed and tried again. This time Shadow snatched the knife out of his hand, glanced at it, and threw it on the floor.

"What did you pay for that sorry weed-cutter, half a copper?" she said impatiently. "You might as well chew through the thong with your teeth for all the edge that'll hold."

"It's the best I've got," Aubry protested.

"Then no wonder you can't bring home a decent day's take. Not that a mark couldn't smell you coming a mile away." Shadow pulled the knife out of her boot sheath and handed it to him. "Here, try that."

Several thongs later, Shadow pronounced Aubry "halfway fit, anyway," and reclaimed her knife, handing him a Sun.

"Now buy yourself a decent blade or two," she sniffed, "and take that toad-stabber back and use it to peel skin off the *real* thief who sold it to you. Or better yet, on your incompetent mentor. Cut the pouch, indeed!"

"Mentor?" Aubry inquired.

Shadow froze midway in the act of putting her knife back in its sheath.

"Didn't Ganrom assign you a mentor?" she asked. "Someone to train you in the basics?" Aubry shook his head. Shadow groaned. "How'd you learn anything?"

Aubry shrugged amiably.

"Trial and error." He grinned. "Luckily for me, not too much error, and no trial yet."

Shadow swore explosively and finished sheathing the knife.

"You mean to tell me," she said slowly, "that that idiot Ganrom just sells you a token and turns you loose? No training, easy picking for any guard, and then because he won't ransom, the guard beats whatever Guild secrets they like out of you at the prison?"

Aubry shrugged again.

"That's about it," he said. "At least that's the way it's been as long as I've been a member. Of course, that's only been a couple of seasons. It may've been different when Evanor was Guildmaster."

"Bet on it," Shadow growled. "It couldn't have been any worse, that's certain.

"Listen, thanks for the Sun, Shady, and the lesson. I'll pay you back," he added humbly, tucking the Sun into his sleeve.

"Call it an exchange of favors." Shadow sighed, then dismissed her annoyance and grinned, giving his belt a tug. "Maybe I'll trade you for a few more lessons in the future."

"Lessons in *what*?" Aubry laughed. Then he sobered. "But I owe you, Shadow, and I won't forget the debt."

"Ah, just find yourself a better place to stay, so I won't have to pick fleas off my hide after." Shadow shrugged amiably. "But I'll tell you what: what if you do me a favor, and yourself one at the same time?"

"What favor?" Aubry asked cautiously. "Forgive me, Shady, but knowing you—"

Shadow poked through her pouch and removed the gold token she'd found on Pim.

"Take this," she said. "*Don't* keep it for yourself, but sell it to some lousy scum of a thief you won't mind seeing take a knife in the back. That way you'll have the gold from the sale, and the credit for taking out a gold-token thief as well."

"How does that help you?" Aubry asked curiously.

"It isn't doing me any good in my pouch." Shadow shrugged. "And if my loyalty's in question, it won't do *my* reputation any good if people think I'm offing other gold-token thieves. Let Ganrom watch someone else for a while."

"Shadow, Ganrom's got more important things to worry about now than you," Aubry said. "You're getting too itchy. The way Vikram's got the Council of Churches stirred up against the Guild now—"

"Well, no wonder," Shadow said exasperatedly. "Look what's been happening. Ganrom should've been keeping a tighter hold on his people. I'm half minded to go challenge him myself."

"You don't understand," Aubry said patiently. "High Priest Vikram has publicly announced that every thief found in the Temple District is going to be blinded and his hands and feet chopped off, and blinding and dismemberment are chancy things to get healed. Around the Guild they're saying that if Ganrom doesn't do something, strike back at the Council of Churches, the Guild's going to be hamstrung."

"And if he *does*, he's as good as inviting the Council of Churches, with the City Council backing them, to retaliate," Shadow said with dawning realization. "Fortune favor me, that Vikram's done a clever setup job!"

Then she frowned.

"But it doesn't make any sense," she said at last. "If that's all there is to it, then why was . . . ?"

"Why was . . . ?" Aubry prompted.

"Oh, no, my tricky friend." Shadow grinned halfheartedly. "I've already divulged enough of my secrets for one tumble. Now I've got to get moving. I've wasted enough time already."

"Wasted?" Aubry grinned, but he sighed disappointedly. "I hoped you'd stay the night. It's already late."

"Maybe another time. I may be a dangerous bedfellow right now, you know," Shadow teased.

"Don't I know, though?" Aubry laughed, rubbing the small of his back. "Well, can I meet you somewhere tomorrow?"

"Mmmm, I've got a lot to do," Shadow said regretfully. "How about dinner at the Horn at sunset?"

"All right."

It was late, indeed, but there was still much to do before

Shadow could return to Argent's house. Hopefully, the information Uncle had given her about jewel merchant Mieron was right; as little as Shadow liked to work on hearsay, there was simply no time to do otherwise. She was running low on funds, and didn't have time for research.

Dalin and his dragon were, of course, long gone, but another warrior had been successful while Shadow was visiting her forest-dwelling kin, and Shadow bought two slabs of dragon meat—one to eat as she walked, the other for her wallet.

Shadow had, of course, seen Mieron's shop in the Mercantile District before, although she hadn't gone in. With the unconscious fact-gathering habit of any good thief, she had made note of the entrances, exits and windows, and knew the guard schedule in the area. She knew that Mieron closed shop early in the evening, since the tavern-going evening crowds were neither the likely nor desired patrons of Mieron's expensive jewelry store. This late, therefore, Mieron was long gone and the crowds were thinning as well, but Shadow opted for rooftops over roads. There were no roof accesses in Mieron's shop, so she let herself down at the rear door and waited for the next guard pass, checking her tools and supplies as she waited and thinking through her strategy once more.

There were three locks on the rear door, and they were all good—good enough, Shadow decided, that it was very unlikely that Mieron would have gone to the additional expense and trouble of putting magical safeguards on the door. Three locks without and his pet drake within would probably be considered enough protection for an entrance to the building. The real hitches would be indoors.

It took Shadow an entire guard pass—nearly an hour—to tickle the first lock open, and by the time she was done she was sweating profusely with worry that the guard might come back before she was done, forcing her to stop mid-lock and rendering all her primary work useless. The lock, however, yielded in time, and Shadow retreated to the roof to wait until the guard passed again.

The second and third locks were easier. Mieron had not been so simple as to buy three similar locks, but there were a limited number of lock types, and the second and third types were more familiar. Mieron had probably counted on the first lock discouraging or delaying anyone trying to gain entrance until a guard showed up. Briefly, Shadow thought that the bracelet would have been handy just at the moment; but where was the sport in that? Having conquered the complicated lock, Shadow could feel like an artist and a specialist, and indeed she was—doing what she was best at.

When the last lock yielded, Shadow again retreated to the roof to wait for the next guard pass. While she waited, Shadow pulled the slab of dragon from her pouch, grimaced, and rubbed it briskly over her arms, legs, and gloved hands. Now, where was the Fortune-be-damned— ah! There was the guard.

To Shadow's consternation, the man chose that particular corner to stop and indulge in a flask and pipe, and Shadow held her breath. Sitting on a roof smelling like dragon, she could be easily found by a sensitive nose. Could Uncle have sold her out? No one else had any idea of her plans, and she hadn't even told Uncle that she would be acting on his information this soon. Then a whiff of smoke reached Shadow, and she almost laughed. The guard's tobacco was every bit as pungent as Aubry's; there was no chance that the guard would be smelling anything else at all.

At last the guard moved on, and Shadow let herself down slowly to the back door. She carefully removed the locks, oiled the door hinges and pulled the door open, stepping into the rear entryway.

The drake was upon her before Shadow saw it, and the small dragonlike creature's weight knocked her sprawling to the floor. Before it attacked, however, it stopped to sniff. Abruptly the drake backed away and waited for Shadow to rise.

Shadow grinned to herself. She knew locks, and she knew drakes. Drakes were, fortunately, not intelligent like their larger dragon-kin, although they were, for their size, every bit as formidable. Shadow smelled like a dragon; therefore, she was a dragon, and to be treated with respect. Additionally, anyone investigating later would smell only the dragon scent, and that was close enough to the scent of the drake that it would take a miraculous nose, indeed, to tell the difference. The loss of her clothes would be worth it.

Shadow's keen night vision made a light unnecessary, although she wished that she had had the opportunity to visit the shop by day and get a better idea of the layout. Still, most places could be eliminated immediately. The front room was too visible from the street windows and the back workroom too obvious. That left only the office.

Walls and ceiling could likewise be eliminated, since Shadow knew the outside dimensions and could compare them with the inside rooms; in any event, the ceiling would have been far too inconvenient. None of the furniture in the room—table, desk, chairs—were large enough to conceal a safe of sufficient size. That left the floor.

Like most buildings in Allanmere, Mieron's shop was built of stone blocks. An initial tapping round of the floor told Shadow that there were no thin or hollow areas; therefore, a whole block had to come up, and that meant a trigger mechanism of some sophistication.

All right, where? Shadow allowed herself a small light in the windowless office to inspect the open part of the floor more closely, but she did not really expect to find anything. No matter how careful Mieron was, one could not move a large block every day without leaving signs that would be visible on open floor. The opening would have to be somewhere that a visitor would not notice a difference in the floor. The table and desk were far too cumbersome for one man to move alone; in fact, the desk appeared to be bolted to the floor, so that left—yes, there it was, a slightly worn-edged stone under the desk's chair.

Right, then. Mieron would come in in the evenings, probably with his arms full of storage boxes, which he would most likely set on the desk for convenience, and then . . . right, bolted to the floor! Shadow ran her fingertips around the edge of the desk, then under the decorative trim. There! A slight click, and the stone started to rise. Just in time, Shadow grabbed the chair before it could topple and crash.

The stone rose on a clever series of pulleys and levers, exposing a steep flight of stone steps leading down. Shadow hesitated, then pulled one of the locks from her pack and used it to wedge the block. Just in case.

Shadow tiptoed carefully down the steps, turning up the wick of her lamp a little more now that there was no chance of the light being seen. The steps were stone, but clean and dry. She followed them down nearly four man-heights before she came to the end—a featureless, dirt-floored alcove containing only a single large chest, prominently padlocked.

Not touching the chest, Shadow knelt before it and withdrew the vial of moly from her pouch. She had no way of telling whether Mieron had been cautious enough to have magical safeguards put on the chest, but it was safer to assume that he had. Carefully, Shadow swabbed the moly on the hinges, lock and around the edge of the chest, and the rest on her gloves.

Given Mieron's precautions so far, Shadow was almost disappointed in the ease of the lock. After all, though, Mieron could scarcely expect anyone else to be opening it, and would not want to go to so much trouble himself on a nightly basis.

Shadow could not suppress a low whistle of awe when she lifted the lid. Set within the chest were shallow storage trays, and within the trays were layer upon layer of her favorite shining, gleaming, and sparkling things. As quickly as caution would permit, Shadow stuffed pouches and sleeves with loose gems. She hesitated over the exquisitely crafted jewelry, then left it regretfully. It would be too recognizable to sell in town, and too dangerous to store or travel with. Loose stones, no matter how precious, could easily be concealed, carried and sold.

Shadow replaced the trays, closed the lid, and shut the padlock, then hurried back up the stairs. The drake was waiting at the top, sniffing curiously at the lock wedged at the edge of the block. Shadow quickly hopped out of the passage, retrieved the lock, and pressed the mechanism, resetting the block in place. She replaced the chair, gave the drake a farewell pat, and extinguished her lamp before she left the room.

She could hear nothing outside the back door, but she took the time to peek out a window before she ventured outside. She replaced all three locks in their proper position, then trotted down the alleys. When she thought she was far enough away, she hurriedly stripped off her dragon-scented clothes and took out her spare clothing from her pack.

She dumped the smelly clothes in someone's garbage fire and hurried back to the main streets, where she noncha-lantly strolled back to Argent's house and let herself in quietly. The elvan shopkeeper was already asleep, and he did not wake when Shadow slid quietly into the bed beside him.

She was utterly exhausted, bruised from the drake's enthusiastic greeting, and a grumbling headache reminded her that she'd overdone it with the Dragon's Blood, but her whirling thoughts would not let her sleep.

How much longer did she dare to stay here with Argent? The fact that Blade's contract had been canceled—and hopefully, that Blade was too annoyed to accept another later—didn't stop Ganrom from hiring anybody else he pleased the second he had the bracelet in his hand. Or do it himself, for that matter; helpless slobs didn't hold the Guild seats as long as he had.

She wouldn't be safe in Allanmere a moment after she handed over the bracelet, or when somebody found out where it was, whichever came first. And if somebody located it before she surrendered it, she'd be as good as writing Donya's mourn-song. Perhaps it had been a bad idea, giving Donya the bracelet, but where else could she have put it? And Donya would never let it spill . . .

Ah, but servants were snoopy, and they would readily talk when offered enough coin; Fortune knew she'd done it often enough in her own time. And possession of the fake bracelet could be every bit as deadly.

And why, why, why was the bracelet so Fortune-be-damned vital? True, it made thieving easy. But any skilled thief could do as well without it as with—ah, but then, Ganrom didn't keep skilled thieves around, did he? So then he needed the bracelet to—to what?

It made no more sense than the goings-on between the Guild and the Council of Churches. If the Council and the Guild were teetering on the brink of open warfare—and they obviously were—what were the dealings between Vikram and Ganrom?

Could Ganrom have been planted in the Guild by Vikram himself, to undermine it in preparation for a final strike from the Council of Churches? That might make sense, in light of the elimination of the more skilled members, and the shoddy management. But if that was the case, the Council of Churches would have been better served to have Ganrom assassinated long before now, and strike while the Guild was crippled and leaderless. Besides, Ganrom might be an idiot and a snake, but he *was* a thief. Why help destroy his own livelihood?

It just didn't make sense.

Shadow thumped her fist into the pillow in frustration, eliciting a mumbled protest from Argent.

What was she to do? If the Council and the Guild erupted into open conflict, it would put her and Donya on opposite sides, and that was something Shadow didn't even like to consider. She knew Donya would never harm her, not even at the price of her own honor and duty, but Shadow refused to put either Donya's loyalties or her own to the test.

The best thing, then, was to get hold of the duplicate bracelet and hand it over to Ganrom as soon as possible—not wait for the seven days—and cut out of Allanmere as quickly as she could, hoping that Ganrom wouldn't send someone after her. She'd take the real bracelet with her so that Donya wouldn't be endangered by keeping it. In any event, who knew? She might need it someday.

For a moment Shadow considered the possibility of sending the duplicate bracelet to Ganrom by someone else. But who? The problem with that thought was that anyone she sent was liable to get killed on the spot, and of the people she trusted, there were none she would put in that kind of danger. No, better to take the risk and deliver it herself. She was better equipped to deal with any kind of treachery Ganrom might be planning, anyway.

Yes, Ganrom might well find a surprise or two in store, dealing with her. Shadow smiled at the thought, and slept.

EIGHT

"Donya left a message yesterday," Argent said conversationally. "She was looking everywhere for you—again."

"What was it?" Shadow asked anxiously.

"Only that she had a package you were expecting." Argent shrugged. "She wanted to know if you'd like to meet her somewhere today."

Shadow thought a moment.

"Will you send a message that I'll meet her at sunset at the palace—the same way I did last time?" she said. "I'm sorry to keep putting you in the middle, but—"

Argent held up a hand to silence her.

"It's no problem," he said firmly. Then he raised an eyebrow.

"What a grim expression," he said lightly. "Is this bad news?"

"Not bad," Shadow said slowly. "Just unexpected. I didn't expect this thing to arrive for a few more days." She sighed.

"And you'll be leaving town, then?" Argent asked abruptly.

Shadow looked up in surprise, then nodded.

"How did you know?" she asked.

"It seemed logical," Argent said gently. "I know you've been in considerable danger. I'll be sorry to see you go. You've been a risky houseguest, but an interesting one, at least." His hand squeezed hers, belying his flippant words.

"You're one of the few things about Allanmere I *will* miss, besides the market." Shadow grinned, but she squeezed his hand back.

"Do you think you'll be back?" Argent asked with studied indifference.

"Probably not for a few—" Shadow stopped, thinking of Donya. She imagined an old woman, crooked and feeble, gnarled hands no longer able to lift a sword.

"Probably not," she finished.

Argent nodded. "Will you stay tonight?"

She'd thought of leaving as soon as she claimed the bracelet and delivered the fake to Ganrom, but—it could be done as well in the morning, and she'd promised to meet Aubry . . . and one last night with Argent would be nice.

"Sure, I'll be here tonight," Shadow said cheerfully. "And you'd better plan on letting Elaria run the shop tomorrow, because I'm not going to let you get any sleep at all."

"Then I'd best get twice as much work done today." Argent laughed, pushing his plate away. "I'll send your message—at sunset, same as last time—and meet you here tonight, then."

His mention of work reminded Shadow that after paying the remainder of Tigan's fee and buying travel supplies, she'd be leaving town with empty pockets if *she* didn't get a little work done. The market was as ripe and profitable as ever; riper, in fact, since Shadow noticed few other thieves in competition. Laying low, no doubt, during the present conflict, and possibly avoiding Shadow herself as a possible troublemaker.

By late afternoon she had accumulated enough gold, gems and small jewelry to see her comfortably to the next large city. She made a brief stop at Uncle's alley, where she gave him all the small coin—why carry the weight?—and wished him well before continuing to the castle.

Donya met her at the garden gate, but instead of going to her room, she led Shadow to one of the outer gardens.

"We'd best stay out here," she said. "I've noticed one or two of the maids getting a little nosy." She drew out a box and handed it to Shadow.

Shadow inspected the duplicate bracelet, shaking her head in awe. It was perfect, even to the inscription inside. Shadow herself could never have seen the difference.

"It's wonderful," Shadow admitted. "Do you have the other one with you?"

Donya's eyes widened.

"I thought you wanted it kept hidden."

"I know." Shadow sighed. "But I think I'd better take it now."

Donya was silent for a long moment.

"You're getting ready to leave, then, aren't you?"

Shadow looked into her friend's troubled eyes and sighed, discarding the story she had been fabricating.

"Yes," she said. "I think it's time I was moving on. I'm going to give Ganrom the fake bracelet. I'll take the real one with me where it won't do any harm."

"Don't you think it would be safer if I kept it?" Donya asked slowly. "Not that I don't trust you," she added hastily. "But if someone finds out that you have it—"

Shadow shook her head.

"It might be safer for me," she said. "But I wouldn't sleep too well at night, wondering if someone'd found out you had it and figuring what they could do to get it from you. No, it's my problem, and I'm content that it stay that way."

Donya sighed, then pushed up her sleeve and, to Shadow's amazement, removed the bracelet from her own wrist.

"Well, what did you expect?" Donya shrugged. "It's the only place I could swear it was safe all the time. I don't think even *you* could've gotten it off me without my knowing it. When are you leaving?"

"I'm hoping to give the fake to Ganrom first thing tomorrow morning," Shadow said. She snapped the fake bracelet onto her right wrist and the real one higher up on the same arm, pulling her sleeve down to cover both. "I'll leave right after, before . . . anyone . . . has time to arrange anything nasty."

Donya laid one hand on Shadow's arm.

"You'll come back to say goodbye, won't you?" she asked, looking into Shadow's eyes.

"Bet on it," Shadow said lightly. "But listen, I'd better give you back your ring, just in case I forget—"

"No, you don't," Donya said immediately, reaching to restrain Shadow from pulling off the ring. "You *weren't* going to come here and say goodbye, were you? No, thanks. You owe me that much, Shady. Bring the ring back tomorrow yourself."

"All right." Shadow sighed. She hadn't wanted to come back; she hated sentimental goodbyes. But—well, all she had to do was say Donya's name backwards and the ring would return itself. She could attach a short note. That would do.

"What about your thousand Suns?" Donya asked her.

"Have them sent to Aspen." Shadow shrugged. "He'd rather I delivered Evanor's assassin, but it's not important enough for me to get killed over." She sighed again. "I don't like leaving you with a mess I may have stirred up, though."

Donya looked at the grass for a moment.

"Shadow," she said slowly, "if you're leaving anyway, can you at least tell me what's been going on?"

"I suppose that's only fair," Shadow said after a moment's thought. "But the truth is, Doe, I really don't know. All I *know* is that after I got hold of that bracelet, everything suddenly exploded. I *know* that Ganrom is the one who sent Blade after me—"

"WHAT?" Donya choked. "Your own Guildmaster—"

"—and that it has something to do with the problems between the Guild and the Council of Churches," Shadow finished with a shrug. "And I know that fellow Derek is involved somehow. But I don't have any other facts to give you. Honestly, Doe, and that's not Guild loyalty talking. Things are building up to a crisis, and I don't like to think what the choices are for the Guild."

"Then there's nothing to be done?" Donya asked bleakly.

"Nothing I can think of," Shadow said, shaking her head. "If either side gives in now, its influence is going to be crippled for good. And if nobody gives in, you're going to have a hell of a bloody fracas on your hands. Stay out of it if you can, is all I can say."

"How can I?" Donya said exasperatedly. "I'm the High Lord's own daughter and heir."

"Get out of town for a while, then," Shadow suggested. "Come with me, if you want. You've always been a traveler. A few good fights, a few good brothels, and you'll be a new person. By the time you get back, it may have all blown over."

Donya slowly shook her head.

"That would be a good idea if I were you, Shady," she

said regretfully. "But I just can't run out on my parents and leave them to deal with this. I can't."

"No, you wouldn't," Shadow said, sighing. "But I had to try."

Donya barely smiled. "I know," she said. "And thanks. But you'd better be going now, before someone sees you here. And you *will* stop by tomorrow morning, right?"

"Bet on it," Shadow said, swallowing hard. "You take care, Doe, you hear me?"

"And you." Donya sighed. "No use telling you to be careful. Well, be lucky, Shady. And don't forget that ring, if you need me before tomorrow."

"No, I won't forget."

Shadow walked with Donya to the gate, but after her friend had turned back, Shadow stood at the gate and watched until Donya vanished into the gardens. A lump rose in Shadow's throat, and she swallowed it down grimly.

"How *do* I get myself into these Fortune-be-damned messes?" she mumbled, realizing that her voice was hoarse. "Well, never mind. What I need is a few cordial drinks with Aubry and a good night's tumble with Argent. That'll set me straight."

Passing through the market, she bought a quill, ink and paper to script a message to Donya and put them in her belt pouch. Better not forget that before she left the city; she didn't know if there might be a distance limitation on the return-spell on the ring.

Shadow looked at the sky and cursed. She'd spent longer with Donya than she'd meant to; Aubry had probably been waiting for her. She hurried to the Three-Spangled Horn, but to her surprise, Aubry was nowhere to be seen. The barkeep knew Aubry, yes, but hadn't seen him tonight. Shadow bought a tankard of ale and sat down, aware that almost every patron was watching her; but to her surprise, almost as soon as she was seated, the customers began to rise and leave until only a few were left.

She waited an hour, then another; then she began to worry.

She pulled five Suns from her purse and slapped them down in front of the surprised barkeep.

"I'm going looking for my friend," she said. "If he comes here, have him wait. If you hear anything, send for me and I'll give you five more Suns, understand?"

The barkeep shrugged and pocketed the money.

"Sure."

Shadow stepped out of the bar, looking for an urchin. Surely Tig and his friends could find——

Someone crashed into her. Shadow reflexively drew a knife, but put it away when she recognized Cris.

"Well, at least *you're* here," she said crossly. "Where in Fortune's name has Aubry gotten to? He was supposed to meet me here quite awhile ago."

Cris' eyes widened. "Haven't you heard?"

"Heard what?" Shadow didn't realize her hands had clenched until she felt the sharp pain of her nails biting into her palms. She took a deep breath and unclenched them.

"Tell me."

"He was caught at the Temple of Urex a little after noon today," Cris mumbled. "They're going to——to——punish him tomorrow at dawn. Right on the temple steps. I knew he was coming here tonight, so I thought——uh——"

"What, by Fortune's left hand, was he doing in the Temple District?" Shadow demanded. "I told him to sell that damned——"

"Your message," Cris said dumbly. "I saw it. It said you were in trouble and to meet you there. I went with him, but I got away. He put up a good fight, he did, and I got away."

"Fortune smite me for a fool," Shadow said bitterly. "Cris, is Ganrom at the Guildhouse now?"

"He ought to be," Cris said confusedly. "But, Shadow, Ganrom won't ransom from—"

"He will this time," Shadow snapped. "I've got what he wants. Look, stay out of this. Just go home and wait there. I don't have time to look out for you, too."

She dashed for Guild Row, leaving Cris standing where he was. For once she cursed rather than blessed the crowded streets that slowed her progress, the laden wagons carelessly left standing in front of shops, the packs of urchins that appeared from nowhere. At last, however, she pushed open the Guildhouse doors; as she expected, Ganrom was there with only a few others.

"Well, if it ain't the smartest thief in the city." Ganrom chuckled. "And what can I do for her tonight?"

"You know why I'm here," Shadow said through clenched teeth. "I want to talk to you—alone."

"Well, now, you don't always get just what you want." Ganrom laughed. "I don't know as I'd feel smart to send my friends away. Seems as if I might want witnesses, eh? You can talk plain, they know what's working."

Shadow's lips compressed, but she nodded.

"All right," she said. "I know what you want. Have them let Aubry go, right now, and you'll have the bracelet."

Ganrom narrowed his eyes.

"Ah, now, missy," he said, grinning. "I ain't such a fool as all that. What's to say you'll get the thing to me when I've done what you wanted?"

Shadow pushed her sleeve up far enough to expose the fake bracelet.

"This says it," she snapped. "Now go on."

Ganrom reached for pen and scroll, then hesitated.

"You've had the thing a powerful long time," he said

easily, putting the pen down. "How do I know you ain't got it un-spelled?"

"Give me a lock," Shadow shrugged. "I'll prove it."

Ganrom gestured at one of the thieves, who pulled the Guild fee box from under the desk. He held it out.

Shadow reached out to touch the lock with her right hand.

"Aufrhyr," she said. There was an audible *snap* as the lock clicked open, and Shadow lifted the lid.

Ganrom reclaimed the box, nodding consideringly.

"Then what's to stop us taking it here and now?" he drawled, leaning back against the counter.

Two knives materialized in Shadow's hands as if by magic.

"These might stop you," she growled. "Look, Ganrom, you aren't a fool. Aubry doesn't mean a damned thing to you and you know it. Now, I can hand the bracelet over and you get it right now, easy. Or you can have your lackeys attack me, and I can kill a few of them, and *maybe* you kill me and get the bracelet—and maybe you don't, and then its gone and you're no better off. Send the damned message. It's cheap enough for you."

Ganrom chuckled, but he reached for the scroll and pen again. He scribbled a short message, then handed it over.

"Let the elf go," it read. "I have the merchandise."

Shadow nodded and handed the scroll back.

"Send it now," she said.

"After you hand over the bracelet," Ganrom corrected, smiling nastily.

"Keep dreaming," Shadow said shortly.

Ganrom shrugged and handed the scroll to one of the thieves.

"Take it," he said. The thief nodded and hurried out the door.

"There you are," Ganrom said easily. "Well?"

Shadow touched the fake bracelet's clasp.

"Aufrhyr," she said, and the clasp snapped open. She took the bracelet off and held it up for Ganrom's inspection, then suddenly threw it over his head. As he and the other thieves roared and reached for it, Shadow turned and fled out the door as quickly as she could.

The thief with the scroll was still in sight, hurrying north. Shadow followed as closely as she dared without being seen. The thief continued north for a couple of blocks, then suddenly turned to look behind him. Shadow ducked behind a barrel, her eyes never leaving him. He slipped into an alley to the west.

Shadow cursed and followed, peeping around the corner. The thief had taken the scroll out of its container and was tearing it into shreds. When that was done, he dropped the scraps onto a refuse pile and sauntered leisurely down the alley, whistling.

"Fortune wither my hair and numb my loins," Shadow swore. "What a damned fool I've been!"

The south end of the market—the flower vendor— Shadow saw only one, a gnarled-looking fellow, and he was packing away his goods for the day.

Shadow grabbed his arm.

"Listen, I need—"

"Hey-ho, there, young snip!" the man growled. "What do you think you're—"

"Black orchids, damn it!"

The man fell silent and scrutinized Shadow through narrowed eyes.

"Black orchids, eh? And would your name be Shadow, miss?"

Shadow nodded.

The man stroked his chin thoughtfully.

"And where'll you be wanting your flowers, then, and when?"

"The Temple of Urex," Shadow snapped. "And I want them yesterday! Do you understand?"

He raised his bushy eyebrows.

"Ah, urgent, is it, eh? Well, for an errand like that—"

"Look, I've got no time for this," Shadow barked. "Here." She pulled the pouch out of her sleeve and thrust it into the man's hand. "Just do it!"

"All right, missy, it'll be done!"

There was no time for caution or crowds. Shadow quickly found a building to climb and leaped from roof to roof, bypassing the market and skirting the Noble District. Still, it took half an hour to reach the edge of the Temple District.

The Temple of Urex was brightly lit, and Shadow was hardly surprised to see the number of men—priests and younger nobles, Derek Batan among them—guarding the entrances. Still, hadn't Argent said something about a dungeon grating? Yes, at the rear.

It took more time than Shadow liked to work her way to the rear of the temple, and more frustrating moments while she timed the guard patrols circling the place. From her perch she could see the grating, set into the ground right up against the temple's foundation.

As soon as she dared, Shadow hurried over to examine the grating. It ran the length of the temple, passing over ten cells. Shadow hissed Aubry's name down five of them before there was a faint reply.

"Shadow?" Aubry's whisper was weak. "Is that you?"

"Bet on it," Shadow whispered back. "Are you all right?"

"Mostly." There was a scuffling sound, and then Shadow could barely see Aubry's face, bruised and pale.

"I'm chained to the wall by one arm," he said. "I can hardly reach the grating. What are you doing here?"

"Getting you out—I hope," she replied. "Listen, are there any guards down there?"

"None here," Aubry said. "They're all up top."

"Good." Shadow hurriedly removed the bracelet from her arm. "Listen, take this. Just put it on, touch the lock and say—"

"This is it?" Aubry said, stunned. "You're going to hand that thing over to me, just like that?"

"Keep quiet, will you?" Shadow hissed. "The word is 'Aufrhyr.' Just touch the lock on your chains and on the door and say it, and they'll open. I'll start a diversion up front to get the guards away, and you'd better get out as quick as you can."

Shadow saw Aubry work the bracelet onto his arm with some difficulty.

"I don't know if I can go very fast," Aubry whispered doubtfully. "My feet are burned and I think my ankle's—"

"Petrified dragon dung, what've they been doing down there?" Shadow muttered. She pulled the pouch over her head and held it over the grating.

"Listen," she said. "I'm going to drop this down. There's a cordial in there that'll—"

"Well, well," a familiar voice said from behind her. "Look who came to visit."

Shadow froze, then turned, moving to hide her hand as she dropped the pouch down into the grating. Ganrom was standing there, Derek and the priest Bobrick beside him.

"Do come in and visit," Bobrick said with a smile. A step sounded behind her, and then a roaring pain in her head obscured whatever else he might have said.

NINE ═══════

Shadow slid into consciousness by slow degrees. Once she partially roused to find herself being searched with callous thoroughness by a huge human, but a cuff across the face sent her reeling back into welcome blackness.

When she woke again, she was shackled to the wall by both wrists and dripping with icy water. Aubry was nowhere to be seen, but Bobrick and Ganrom were standing not far away. Two guards were just leaving, buckets in hand.

"Welcome back, missy." Ganrom grinned.

Bobrick wasted no time on sarcasm.

"Who was with you?" he demanded.

Shadow shook her head, causing arrows of pain to shoot through her.

"What?" she murmured, feigning more confusion than she felt.

"You had an accomplice," Bobrick said flatly. "Someone who broke your little friend out while we were capturing you. You may as well tell us who it was. We'll have them

163

in a little while anyway. They can't have gotten out of the District."

"I don't know what you're talking about," Shadow said adamantly.

"Look, the damned kid don't matter," Ganrom snapped. "You got her, ain't you? What matters is this." He held up the duplicate bracelet.

"Why, what's the matter?" Shadow asked innocently, her eyes wide.

Ganrom scowled. It took him only three steps to reach her, and his blow sent her head reeling back to crack against the stone of the cell. Her vision doubled, then trebled.

"This ain't the bracelet," he said, his face close to hers. "Now, you want to tell us nice where the thing is, or you want to do it the hard way?"

"Hit me again if it makes you feel better," Shadow said as lightly as she could. "Hit me twenty times, if you like. And tomorrow, when you all haul me out to the temple steps, I'll shout it to the world that you—"

Bobrick's face suddenly loomed in her vision.

"What makes you think, my dear," he said gently, "that you'll ever leave the temple?"

"You can blind me and cut off my hands and feet, but you can't kill me," Shadow said sweetly. "And don't think there aren't plenty who'll find out if you break the law. There's others who know where I went—"

"Ah, but will it matter?" Bobrick asked, raising his eyebrows.

"Maybe not to you," Shadow said as levelly as she could. Her head throbbed abominably, and her vision blurred with each throb. "But Vikram can't afford the scandal. He won't allow anything that'll endanger his influence now."

"Vikram?" Bobrick repeated. "Ah, Vikram. Poor Vikram.

What a sad story. He'll be at the castle at a function until after midnight, arguing with the High Lord again—vainly, I'm sure. Tonight after Vikram returned, a thief broke into the temple to rescue some two-copper cutpurse, and, do you know, in the process, the thief killed Vikram. We tortured the thief, of course, and executed her—as is our right under the law, when dealing with an assassin, you know."

Assassin—Blade! Was she near? And Aubry? Had he gotten away cleanly?

Thoughts pushed through the miasma of Shadow's pain, and slowly events began to fall into place.

"It never was Vikram, then, was it?" she said hoarsely. "It was you all along, Bobrick. Ganrom, you poor, pathetic fool."

"Oh, who's the fool?" Ganrom chuckled. "As I see it, you're the one in a bit of difficulty, eh?"

Shadow swallowed hard and tried to force her voice level.

"Don't you see?" she said. "Bobrick wants Vikram out of the way, and he's set the Guild up to take the fall. No matter what happens to me, when Vikram's assassinated, the Council of Churches will—"

"Oh, no, see, it's you as don't understand." Ganrom grinned. "It's Vikram's been the trouble all along, see? Bobrick's been doing business with me some time, missy, and it's profited us both, and when Vikram's out of the way, see, we won't have no more problems."

"Oh, you idiot, you can't really believe that." Shadow groaned. "What the hell do you think he needed the bracelet for? He's been using it—"

"I think that's enough," Bobrick said mildly. "I think the real issue here is where you've hidden that very bit of evidence. Bandied about, you see, it could cause us quite a little trouble, and I think you'd be wise to tell us now and spare yourself a good bit of pain. We needn't torture you, you see. If you were caught in the scuffle with Vikram, it's very possible that you were killed before you could be captured. It's all up to you, you see."

Shadow's mind spun furiously. Vikram obviously wasn't dead yet; they'd have to wait until the crowds outside were gone, for fear of discovery. If Aubry had gotten away, he'd be going for help, perhaps even to Donya, or more likely, to Argent. Either of them would know what to do. She needed time—

She smiled sweetly.

"I gave it to Aubry."

"Oh, yes," Ganrom sneered. "Right, missy, you done gave it to some two-copper thief. I know as you didn't have it before, see? Try a better one."

She took a deep breath, screwed up her courage, and spat full in Bobrick's face.

The Temple of Urex employed skilled people. Artisans, in fact, in their own area of specialty. Despite her position, Shadow had to appreciate the enthusiasm with which some of them went about their work. It seemed like a decade, but was probably less than an hour before she gasped out a confession that, yes, she'd hidden the bracelet—it was buried just outside the Sun Gate—she'd hidden it when she'd left town, just in case, and bought a duplicate that was cheaply spelled to work only the once. No, no one else knew where she'd hidden the real one; who could she trust?

They didn't trust *her*, though; she'd counted on that. She was returned to her cell and shackled there (although her guards were kind enough to leave her left wrist, which was broken anyway, free) while men were sent to check the location she'd given. For a time she wavered in and out of reality, then blackness came as a welcome friend.

* * *

"Well, well. What a fortunate meeting."

For a moment, Shadow almost panicked—was Ganrom back so soon? But the voice was female. Shadow forced her eyes open.

Blade stood in front of her, wavering in her blurry vision.

"How did you get in here?" Shadow croaked.

Blade chuckled, a dry little chuckle that made Shadow shiver.

"I go where I will," she said. "Did you summon me to ask me about my trade secrets?"

"No." Shadow blinked hard and her vision cleared somewhat. "How safe are we? What time is it?"

"For perhaps an hour, and it is nearly midnight." Blade's eyes narrowed. "Have you a bargain for me, or not?"

Shadow had to laugh at that, although it made her broken ribs hurt viciously.

"Does it look like I have any money on me?" she gasped. "I gave most of it to your messenger, and the guards took everything else I had."

"I am not concerned with your coin." Blade's face was blank. "Give me a name. Ganrom?"

"No. Bobrick."

One black eyebrow arched gracefully.

"Indeed. You've learned more than I thought."

Shadow coughed, tasting blood.

"You knew?"

"Of course." Blade shrugged. "What matter to me? Let them all kill each other. They've kept me well in work."

Shadow shook her head. No matter.

"What do you want?" she croaked. "My life you could've had before."

"Ah, no." Blade shook her head, smiling regretfully. "Much as I might enjoy that, I see that you stand at the focus from which larger ripples spread. Three decades is my price."

"What?" Shadow shook her head in confusion, sending hot nails of pain through her temples. "Three decades of what?"

"Three decades of your life." Blade drew the black dagger from her belt, toyed with it. "Ordinarily my price would be but one; however, I find myself in—shall we say—a favorable bargaining position. So. Three decades, and I will even give a bonus."

She tossed a bundle at Shadow's feet—her confiscated belongings, including her knives, tools, bottle of Dragon's Blood . . . and Donya's ring.

"All right," Shadow croaked. "Three decades. I don't suppose you'd like to throw in getting me out of this manacle?"

"You have your tools there," Blade mocked.

"And I have four broken fingers and a broken wrist here," Shadow returned, weakly lifting her free hand. "Come on. I'll throw in five more years, eh?"

"Unfortunately three decades is the most I can claim in one payment." Blade shrugged and touched the tip of the black dagger to the lock. It snapped open and Shadow collapsed to the floor, groaning as the impact jarred every injury.

"I don't suppose you saw what happened to Aubry," Shadow said, gasping, slowly gathering her belongings.

"I have better ways to pass my time than chasing escaped thieves," Blade sneered. "Have we a bargain or not?"

"I said we did." Shadow weakly pushed herself to her feet. "So what now?"

Blade held out one black-gloved hand.

"Your hand," she said.

Shadow looked at her own swollen hands. She shrugged

and held out her left hand. It had four broken fingers and the wrist was cracked; what more could Blade do to it?

Blade took the hand with surprising gentleness and bent over it, briefly pressing her lips to Shadow's palm. Shadow felt nothing, but when Blade released her hand, there was a small black mark on the skin, shaped somewhat like a dagger.

The black eyes sparkled and Blade smiled, a cold smile.

"I thank you for your business," she said lightly. "And I will be about mine. As to your elf lover, I know nothing— but perhaps this was what you were looking for in any wise. It was caught in the grating."

She tossed Shadow's small neck-pouch at her feet, and before the stunned elf could say anything more, was gone.

Shadow gaped a minute more, then shook herself. There was no time to stand there gawking. Vikram might have already left the castle. How much time had passed? Impossible to tell.

Shadow awkwardly worked the small pouch open, and then wasted even more time prying the vial open with her teeth. She took a ginger swallow of the liquid, but dared not wait for any effect. As quickly as her abused hands would allow, she took the pen, ink and paper and clumsily penned a short note: "Keep Vikram there under guard. Watch for assassins. STAY THERE! S." She rolled the paper tightly until it would fit through the ring.

"Aynod," she said, and the ring vanished. Maybe, if Fortune's left hand was through belaboring her, it might reach Donya in time to do some good.

By the time she had finished that task, she began to feel a tingling through her body, hot but not unpleasant. She could only hope that the starleaf tincture worked quickly; there was no time to waste.

The door was locked. Blade's bizarre sense of humor, or

had she walked through it like a spirit? Shadow would have
as readily believed either supposition. Cursing at the pain,
she worked her tools out of their leather pouch and cursed
again with frustration at the time it took to pick the simple
lock. At last, however, the door swung open and Shadow
limped out. There were two guards lying in the hall, their
throats slit.

It was hard to tell, but her breathing seemed to be easing
a bit and her head was slowly clearing. Shadow debated
with herself for a moment, then swallowed a second sip of
the tincture.

What now? She had the run of the dungeon for the
moment, but she could hear people moving around above,
and Ganrom and Bobrick would be back before long. She
was in no shape to fight her way out of a crowd of guards,
but ordinary priests—maybe. She shook her head, pleased
that it hurt only a little, and headed for the stairs.

Immediately she flattened herself beside the door, glancing frantically about. There were footsteps approaching
down the stairs, certainly more than one person. There was
nowhere to hide except in the temple's "questioning" room
or one of the empty cells; quickly Shadow opted for the
former and ducked inside, shutting the door but for a crack
to peer through.

A hot glow was beginning in her stomach, and Shadow
wondered about the wisdom of her second dose of the
tincture. Could it poison her?

Bobrick and Ganrom, followed by three guards, stepped
into the dungeon. There had been no time or opportunity to
hide the dead guards, and Shadow's cell door stood open.

"Blight her, where could she have gone?" Ganrom
shouted as the guards searched the cells. "I'd have vowed
she couldn't move a step!"

The glow was turning to a wave of hot energy that pulsed

through Shadow, not unpleasant but frightening in its intensity. Shadow panted, feeling the energy swell within her as if it would burst out.

"Softly, softly," Bobrick growled, pacing. "She obviously had help. Maybe the thief who escaped earlier or the accomplice who helped him, who knows? It doesn't matter. She must be down here somewhere unless she was magicked out; the men above would've seen—"

He was interrupted by a scream, dimly heard from above, followed by more.

"Go see what that is," Bobrick snapped to one of the guards, who immediately ran up the stairs.

"In any event," Bobrick finished, "she couldn't get far in her condition. There's no other way."

The pain was gone now; Shadow could feel nothing but the swelling heat and energy, as if she'd eaten a whole handful of swiftberries—

"The grates are all intact," one of the guards said. "She ain't in any of the cells."

The other guard moved toward Shadow, grasping the handle of the door.

"Only one place left," he shrugged. "If she ain't in here, she plumb floated through the—"

Shadow moved without conscious thought as the door opened, and the guard stopped in mid-sentence, staring dumbly down at the dagger driven up under his sternum. He looked from the dagger to Shadow, groaned, and slowly slumped forward.

The other guard was on her immediately. His momentum slammed Shadow back against the wall, and she heard ribs grate, but she was beyond pain. Her body sang with strength, and before the guard could raise his sword she had danced lithely aside. Another dagger leaped into her hand and she laughed, easily dodging his swing.

The guard's face clouded with rage, but he restrained himself, watching her movements as he planned a more careful attack. He moved back a bit, easily within sword range but out of reach of Shadow's daggers.

He swung again and Shadow ducked under the blow, giving his leg a token cut as she passed. She moved for the door but he cut her off, and Shadow was forced to jump and then roll as a backhand slash caught her off guard.

Damn him, he wasn't giving her time to set up for a throw, and his sword kept her too far out of reach for a stab. He was closing in again—

Shadow's back struck the rack behind her. Immediately she jumped up and back, rolling over the wooden surface to put it between herself and the guard. Her very blood sang, and in the moment it took him to reach the rack, Shadow's hand had flashed forward. The guard gave a hoarse scream, pawed at the dagger protruding from his eye socket, and fell.

Shadow left him where he lay, not pausing to retrieve her dagger. As she expected, Bobrick and Ganrom were nowhere to be seen in the dungeon, but she could hear more shouting and frantic footsteps above.

No time for subtlety. Shadow drew another dagger and dashed up the stairs on a wave of drug-born power and found, to her surprise, that the footsteps were being made not by guards, but by white-robed priests, scurrying here and there in frantic haste. The situation struck her as deliciously amusing, and it seemed quite logical to stop and laugh at them, until she divined the cause.

The temple was burning.

In the second it took Shadow to assess the situation, she was nearly trampled by a cadre of terror-stricken novices, bowled over by two fat initiates, and flattened by a falling urn. In her intoxicated euphoria she found even this delightful, but almost whimsically she decided to seek Bobrick and Ganrom rather than stay for the spectacle.

The billowing smoke sobered her to some extent. Where, by Fortune's left hand, was she in this damned place? She followed the fleeing priests, trying to avoid the main rush as well as falling debris. There were the temple steps ahead of her—

Coughing and choking, Shadow stumbled over some large object on the steps and tumbled painfully down the marble slabs, but even this could not stop her. She was instantly on her feet again, and spared the cause of her tumble a disgusted glance—

—only to find herself looking at the very, very dead body of Bobrick the priest. His eyes were open, and the look on his face was truly horrendous. His body had been opened in a single stroke from crotch to throat.

"Shadow!"

A hand grabbed her arm, and Shadow spun with her knife, only to pull back the blow just in time before it slammed into Aubry's throat.

"Fortune damn you, don't *do* that!" Shadow growled.

"That's the thanks I get?" Aubry said, rolling his eyes. "She tries to stab me and curses me. Does she ask if I'm all right? Do I get a kiss for my trouble? Does she even—"

"Never mind! Never mind!" Shadow snapped. "Where's Ganrom?"

"I saw him heading back for the Guild at a full run," Aubry said. "I don't think you can catch him now—"

"Just watch me," Shadow said grimly. She glanced around.

A crowd was gathering, including several of the City Guards. More than one of the latter were heading for them and Shadow strongly doubted that they were coming to her rescue.

Dragging Aubry behind her, Shadow ducked into the crowd of fleeing priests and interested onlookers, elbowing her way through and ignoring the shouts of the guards behind her. Then she saw what she wanted just ahead.

"Hey! That's a guardsman's horse!" Aubry protested as Shadow slashed through the knotted reins with a single stroke, but he lifted her up and quickly mounted behind her. "We're going to get in a lot of trouble for this, you know!"

"More than we're in now?" Shadow grinned, digging her heels into the horse's side.

Frightened by the fire and the noise, the animal needed no urging. People dodged aside as the horse bolted toward the outer edge of the Temple District, through the outskirts of the Noble District, and into the market.

"Hold on!" Shadow shouted back to Aubry. "This is liable to get a little tricky!"

"Oh, you think so?" Aubry shouted back as he bounced wildly up and down on the horse's rump.

The horse plunged recklessly through the market, upsetting smaller stands and dodging larger ones. Fortunately, due to the late hour, the market was all but deserted, but what folk there were screamed and threw themselves out of the way. Shadow's legs slammed into wooden supports and building walls, and Aubry was cursing behind her. Shadow clung grimly to the flowing mane with her good hand and wished she'd been a little more conscientious in dropping her coins in the cups at Fortune's temple.

The energy wave provided by the starleaf tincture was slowly ebbing, and Shadow was beginning to again feel the pain of her injuries, although the pain was less and she could move more freely. She was healing, if slowly.

"You didn't get to the castle, did you?" Shadow called back to Aubry.

"I tried," Aubry yelled back. "I couldn't get near

it—there were guards all over and the place was in an uproar and they wouldn't let me through—"

Then Vikram might already be dead, if an assassin had gotten through at the castle. But Bobrick had said they were waiting for him to return to the temple . . .

"So then what?" Shadow yelled.

"So then I went to Argent's shop, but it was closed for the night," Aubry called. "And I didn't know where his house was, so I sent a messenger and went for Cris—"

"DUCK!" Shadow screamed, flattening herself against the horse's neck as they passed under a balcony. Aubry's head smacked into her back and he swore, but his grip did not slacken.

"Damn, but I hate these moving mountains," Shadow added. "What was Cris for?"

"He's a firebug!" Aubry shouted.

"Huh?" The strengthening effects of the starleaf tincture was almost gone now, and Shadow was beginning to feel dangerously tired. Desperately, she clutched the horse's mane tighter.

"He—ouch!—started the fire. It was a—yow! Watch it, will you?—distraction while I tried to get you out! Hey, watch the horse, will you?"

They were turning onto Guild Row. Shadow could see a small crowd gathering in front of the Guildhouse, including several warriors—Dalin among them—and one unmistakable figure. Donya ran over to lift Shadow down from the horse.

"Grief, Shady, what *happened* to you?" Donya gasped, horrified, when she got a good look at her friend.

"I'll live," Shadow said, panting. She was reeling with exhaustion, but there was no time for rest. Hurriedly, she pulled out the vial of starleaf tincture and took a large swallow, trying not to imagine what it might do to her.

"Where's Ganrom?" she demanded as she replaced the vial in its pouch. An ominous fire was already starting in her stomach.

"I don't know," Donya said. She looked around, locating a bench, and helped Shadow to it. "I got your message, and as soon as I saw things straight at the castle, I came right here with some friends. I didn't know where else to look. Here, let me take care of some of this."

"I'll go for a healer," Dalin offered, disappearing into the crowd.

Almost immediately, Aubry materialized beside Shadow.

"He's coming now," Aubry panted. "I had some of the street kids watching out."

"Never mind now," Shadow said, pushing Donya's hands away. "It'll wait."

Ganrom, followed by two or three brawny thieves, pushed his way through to the front of the Guildhouse. He stopped in amazement when he saw Shadow, then grinned.

"So you made it out, eh?" he chuckled. "Got to admire that, you know. I'd as soon settle you myself, anyway."

Before Shadow could move, Donya had drawn her sword and stepped in front of her. Ganrom's jaw dropped as he recognized her.

"I'm here in the name of the High Lord and Lady of Allanmere," Donya said through clenched teeth. "And on behalf of the royal house and the City Council—"

"No." Shadow stumbled forward and put her hand on Donya's arm. "Stay out of it, Doe."

"I can't do that, Shady," Donya said flatly. "Look at you. Guild or no Guild, this is a city matter now."

"I said, *stay out of it*, Doe," Shadow said, her eyes boring into Donya's. "I mean it. It has to be me."

"Shadow—"

"*No*. You owe me this one, Doe."

Shadow's gaze did not waver, and finally Donya stepped back and sheathed her sword.

"All right," she said quietly. "If you have to."

"I have to." Shadow barely smiled. "Besides, you're the only witness in this neighborhood that a judge would believe, anyway."

Ganrom chuckled at their argument.

"Well, what's it to be?" he called. His eyes swept over Shadow's battered form, and he grinned again. "You going to come forward or just talk me to death? Knife to knife, that's how it's done in the Guild, midget."

Shadow was trembling now with suppressed anger and the energy of the drug, building until she was unsure if her body would hold it. What if the stuff burnt her gut out? What if—?

"I'm ready when you are," she said, stepping forward. "Knife to knife it is."

She waited until Ganrom drew two knives, but drew only one herself—her left hand still could not clutch with any strength. Then she waited until the crowd drew back to clear a circle around her and Ganrom.

As Shadow had suspected, Ganrom was no novice. He did not move in but waited for her, assessing her weaknesses. He was tired—he'd run across town on foot—but, Shadow guessed, nowhere near his limit. He was fit enough, and hardly even breathing hard. She, on the other hand, was injured and exhausted, and shaking badly now from the drug. She hoped that its energy could sustain her long enough to best Ganrom—if she could.

Ganrom let her cover most of the distance before he closed, leading with a feint to the right while his left-hand dagger flashed. Shadow barely parried, having to block his wrist with her own; had the tincture not been blocking her pain, the jar on her broken fingers might have incapacitated her.

No time to be subtle; with her injuries, she could not hope to outlast Ganrom. Her parries only just deflected his cuts, and she could manage no offensive when she had to engage both his knives against her one. He knew she was skilled, he knew the extent of her weaknesses—more than she knew of him. So she'd have to come up with something he wouldn't expect.

Ganrom moved in, and this time Shadow's parry came a moment too late. His dagger drew a line of white fire along her ribs. From behind her, Shadow heard a gasp, then heard Aubry's voice, strained and trembling, saying, "Stay out of it, Lady Donya."

Cut, slash, parry, cut—the pattern wove on, and Shadow could feel the drug's energy fading faster this time. Something he wouldn't expect, something—

The cut burned more than it should. Poisoned? No wonder the drug was fading! Shadow clenched her teeth as Ganrom's dagger hilt battered her aching fingers, then forced an awkward parry—

Abruptly Ganrom lunged hard to the right, engaging Shadow's knife, and then sank his left-hand knife to the hilt in Shadow's shoulder. She hardly felt the pain as heat flared in her again, and she heard Donya's agonized cry behind her—

In a motion almost too quick for the eye to follow, Shadow whipped the dagger from her hip with her injured left hand and jammed it upward as hard as she could, ignoring the crack as fingers and wrist gave way, to bury its length under Ganrom's breastbone.

Ganrom's eyes widened more in surprise than pain, and he gave a small, startled croak . . . then slumped forward onto Shadow, his blood spilling warmly over her.

Shadow lay where she was, wheezing, uncaring of the mess of Ganrom's blood soaking through her clothes or his weight on her cracked ribs, only of the growing fire in her shoulder and the incredible agony of her hand. She was dimly aware of Donya flinging the man's body aside like an empty skin and probing the area around the knife carefully before pulling it out of her shoulder—ah, Fortune, that HURT—but when Donya started to lift her, she managed to shake her head.

"Dalin's brought a healer," Donya was saying quickly. "We'll have you right in a few hours, Shady—"

"No," Shadow muttered. "Help me up."

Donya shook her head briskly.

"Whatever it is, it'll wait, Shady. Fortune, Aubry, you look almost as bad, but can you give me a hand with her—"

"No," Aubry said suddenly. "She's right, my lady. Let me have her."

As Donya gaped, Aubry carefully draped Shadow's right arm over his shoulders.

"Can you walk?" he said gently. "It isn't far."

"Bet on it." Shadow grinned gamely. "Let's go."

Careful not to squeeze her injured ribs, Aubry half-carried Shadow over to Ganrom's body. The crowd fell silent as Aubry nudged the body over onto its back with his foot, then gently eased Shadow down beside it.

"Go on," he said. "You have to do it."

In the end, though, Shadow's fingers were too twisted and swollen, and Aubry had to help her lift off the Guildmaster's sigil and place it around Shadow's neck.

"I offer my oath to my new Guild—ah, Guildmistress," Aubry said with a grin, and bent to carefully kiss Shadow's hand.

Shadow cleared her throat.

"I accept your oath," she said.

A stunned silence followed. Then, one by one, the Guild members began to come forward to offer their oaths.

There were no challenges.

"So as I figure it, it was Bobrick who backed Ganrom when he took the seat," Shadow explained. "I thought it was funny that an aspiring Guildmaster would have had enough money to buy Evanor's death. Evanor was a seasoned thief, you know, and a damned good mage as well, and no assassin would take on a job like that for less than several thousand Suns. Not to mention the bad reputation that assassinating such a popular figure would bring to the Aconite Circle."

"But why did Bobrick want Ganrom in the seat?" Donya asked. "Why not just kill Evanor and be done with it?"

"For the same reason that they were working so hard to get me out of the way," Shadow told her. "Back before Ganrom took the seat, there were actually *four* big voices in Allanmere—the City Council, the Council of Churches, the Guild, and the elves. But the elves supported the Guild, you see—one of the few professions that really fits in with the elvan lifestyle—and made it powerful. Bobrick needed Ganrom, a human, to take over the Guild and discredit it so that it'd lose the elvan support. Otherwise the elves would have allied with the Guild against the Council of Churches, and he would've been no better off than when he'd started. Pass me some more wine, would you?"

Argent poured half a mug and handed it over.

"I think that's all you should have," he said gently. "Healer Auberic said not to drink too much until the last of the starleaf tincture was out of your system."

Shadow grimaced and drained the mug, wincing a little as her bandaged fingers curled around the handle.

"But how did Bobrick get Ganrom to go along with it?"

Aubry asked. "He was a sorry Guildmaster, sure, but he didn't act like he was *trying* to destroy the Guild."

"He wasn't." Shadow shrugged, grimacing again as her tightly wrapped ribs protested. "Ganrom was a poor, sorry fool who didn't know he was being played for a pawn. Bobrick pretended sympathy and helped Ganrom gain the seat. Ganrom was good for the job because he'd make a poor Guildmaster, because he was inexperienced enough that he could be fooled, and because his connections with the Aconite Circle would be handy. Destroying the Guild was only one of Bobrick's aims. What he really wanted was to get Vikram assassinated. Then, as Vikram's second-in-command, he'd take Vikram's place at the head of the Council of Churches. With the Guild out of the way, and the elves alienated, the only other voice in the city would be the City Council—and by using the Guild to get Vikram out of the way, the City Council would be sympathetic to the Council of Churches anyway. It would be years before the Guild could bring up its power again, if ever."

"So Bobrick played Vikram and Ganrom against each other," Donya mused, "egging Vikram on against the Guild, while secretly pretending to support Ganrom, all the while convincing Ganrom that the Guild's troubles would be over if Vikram was out of the way and Bobrick in his place. Then, when Ganrom finally had Vikram assassinated, Bobrick, as head of the Council of Churches, would be justified in launching a real strike against the Guild— killing Ganrom, the one person who knew his plans, in the process."

"But where does the bracelet come into this?" Aubry scowled. "It seemed so important."

"It *was* important," Shadow agreed. "Remember who had it?"

"Derek had it," Donya remembered. "But what does he

have to do with it? I thought you said it was Ganrom who got it when Evanor was assassinated."

"That's right." Shadow nodded. "The bracelet was Bobrick's price for his support of Ganrom. It was Bobrick who engineered the clumsy thefts in the Temple District, trying to discredit the Guild. He hired flunkies—minor thieves who otherwise couldn't afford a gold token—through Derek, who would lend them the bracelet to make the thefts. If they were caught, Bobrick would retrieve the bracelet. Derek was also a go-between for Bobrick and Ganrom. Ganrom didn't know that Bobrick was using the bracelet to frame the Guild for the temple thefts; why should he know? He didn't bother to keep track of his thieves or supervise them."

"But why were *you* so important?" Argent asked. "Forgive me, Shadow, but even when you acquired the bracelet, the damage had already been done, hadn't it?"

Shadow shook her head.

"Bobrick still hadn't pushed Vikram into a decisive strike, and he needed a decisive strike to make Ganrom act. When I stole the bracelet, Bobrick knew that it was the one clue to what he'd been doing. If Ganrom found out, the whole thing was off—and a skilled enough thief might figure it out, and tell her Guildmaster what was going on. So I had to die before I could figure it out. Also," Shadow added, "neither Bobrick nor Ganrom knew for sure that I wasn't an agent of the local elves, trying to return the Guild to its previous status by unseating Ganrom. I gave my own origins away at the Three-Spangled Horn—idiotically enough, I practically broadcast it with that dance. You always were smarter than me, Doe.

"When I stalemated them by hiding the bracelet, Bobrick came up with a better idea," Shadow continued. "Why not use me, a local elf and a thief as well, as a scapegoat for

Vikram's assassination? Ganrom would be glad enough to get me out of the way that he'd cooperate, and if it was said that I was the one who killed Vikram, that would be plenty of justification for the Council of Churches to crush the Guild. Again, that didn't occur to Ganrom because he believed Bobrick was his ally."

"So I was bait to capture you?" Aubry asked, eyes wide. Shadow nodded.

"Right. Ganrom knew we were friends, and he knew that by having you captured, he could get me to hand over the bracelet. He and Bobrick also knew I'd come after you when you weren't released, and were ready for me. And even if they didn't manage to capture me, they already had you—also a thief and a local elf—and you would've done almost as well for Bobrick's purposes."

Donya shook her head slowly.

"That was some plan," she said with wonder. "And it almost worked, didn't it? But I still don't understand why you didn't let me kill that pox-ridden idiot Ganrom. He almost slaughtered you, Shady!"

"It had to be me, that's the way it works," Shadow explained patiently. "You weren't a thief; you couldn't claim the seat. If you'd killed Ganrom, the Guild would've been up for grabs and you would have just done Bobrick's work for him—crippling the Guild, anyway, and *without* resolving the conflicts between the Guild and the Council of Churches. Vikram would have squashed the next Guildmaster underfoot like a pesky bug. But I'm a local elf, so I'll have the elvan backing. I've got some support in the Guild—" she winked at Aubry, "—and I'm your friend. Vikram won't dare take any action right away, especially when he learns that I'm the one who kept him from being assassinated and killed Ganrom, which I'd much appreciate you telling him. He's probably never going to let up on the Guild, but it'll give me a little breathing space."

"Space to do what?" Argent asked curiously.

"To get the Guild back on its feet." Shadow shrugged. "To mend its reputation, maybe, and to draw the elvan support back in. To get some kind of a reliable system working. To clean up that pesthole of a Guildhouse. And then to find somebody else to take on the Fortune-be-damned Guild so I'm off the hook."

"What I can't understand," Donya said, "is how you managed to kill Bobrick. You weren't in much shape for Ganrom, and the tincture had been working for a while then. So how did you manage Bobrick?"

Shadow grinned and rubbed the palm of her left hand.

"Just call it paying an old debt," she said mysteriously. "I've got to have a *few* trade secrets. After all, look at the headaches I'm in for. Guildmistress, Fortune favor me! If I didn't know better, Doe, I'd swear that you'd conjured up the whole thing yourself."

"I can't deny I'm pleased with the way things worked out," Donya admitted. "But don't blame me. You're the one who stole the damned bracelet, after all."

"But whatever *did* happen to the bracelet?" Argent asked.

Aubry burst out laughing, then pushed his sleeve up to display the object of the discussion.

"I've still got it." He chuckled. "The Mother Forest knows I *tried* to hide it, but I couldn't get the leaf-rotting thing off my arm! Shadow never told me how."

Everyone laughed heartily, and it was some moments before Shadow could manage to gasp out an explanation to Aubry. She took the bracelet back.

"But what'll you do with it?" Donya asked dubiously.

"Look at all the trouble it's made already. Don't you think you should get rid of it?"

"Get *rid* of it?" Shadow laughed. "After all the trouble I've gone through for this Fortune-be-damned thing? What's the matter, Doe, don't you trust me?" Her wide eyes sparkled innocently.

"I can't think of a better hand to wear it," Argent said gallantly.

"Fortune save us all," Donya groaned, covering her face with her hands.

"*I* think this calls for a drink to our new Guildmistress," Aubry said diplomatically. He saw the bottle of Dragon's Blood on Shadow's nightstand and reached for it. "Hey, what's this stuff? Can we try it?"

Shadow grinned.

"Bet on it," she said.